Augustus W. Dubourg

Angelica

A romantic drama in four acts

Augustus W. Dubourg

Angelica
A romantic drama in four acts

ISBN/EAN: 9783337049324

Printed in Europe, USA, Canada, Australia, Japan

Cover: Foto ©Andreas Hilbeck / pixelio.de

More available books at **www.hansebooks.com**

AUGUSTUS W. DUBOURG

ANGELICA

ROMANTIC DRAMA

LONDON

RICHARD BENTLEY AND SON,

NEW BURLINGTON STREET

Publishers in Ordinary to Her Majesty the Queen

1892

ANGELICA

ROMANTIC DRAMA IN FOUR ACTS

NOTE.

ANGELICA

Romantic Drama in Four Acts

BY

A. W. DUBOURG

AUTHOR OF "FOUR ORIGINAL PLAYS," ETC.
JOINT AUTHOR (WITH TOM TAYLOR) OF THE COMEDY "NEW MEN
AND OLD ACRES," ETC.

LONDON
RICHARD BENTLEY AND SON
Publishers in Ordinary to Her Majesty the Queen
1892

E.V.

" But 'tis Reynolds' way
   From wisdom to stray,
   And Angelica's whim
   To be frolic like him."
            Dr. Goldsmith (impromptu lines).

CHARACTERS.

SIR JOSHUA REYNOLDS . .	President of the Royal Academy.
MR. BARTOLOZZI, R.A. .	Engraver, etc.
MR. KAUFFMANN . .	Father to Angelica.
JOHN NORTHCOTE . .	A lad from Devonshire.
HIS EXCELLENCY THE SWEDISH AMBASSADOR.	
COUNT STROSSMAN .	First Secretary to the Swedish Embassy.
HANS .	Servant to Strossman.
FERSEN . . .	Valet to Strossman.
BOW STREET OFFICER.	
SHERIFF'S OFFICER.	
FOOTMAN TO LADY MARGARET FORBES.	

MISS ANGELICA KAUFFMANN, R.A.	
LADY MARGARET FORBES .	In love with Sir Joshua Reynolds.
MISS REYNOLDS . .	Sister to Sir Joshua Reynolds.
SERVANT TO ANGELICA.	
GUESTS, MOCK GUESTS, CROWD, BOW STREET OFFICERS.	

ACT I.

"SHE STOOPS TO CONQUER."

SCENE.

Large room in Lady Margaret Forbes' house in Grosvenor Square, used as a studio. Entrance to room, R.; entrance to library, L., large window at end of room looking out into a town garden. Easel and sitter's chair in centre of room—small table near window with engraver's appliances.

Bartolozzi discovered in conversation with Kauffmann.

BARTOLOZZI.

Excellently well lodged, friend Kauffmann—good north light for work—ah! and a convenient table for your cameo-cutting and seal-engraving. Comfortable quarters in all respects, I'll be bound.

KAUFFMANN.

Lady Margaret is very kind to us—loves Angelica like a sister—would make us stay here till Angelica can get settled in the house she has taken in Golden Square. She loves painting and artists, does my lady—her love is greater than her art; but her art is good enough for a grand lady—though there's no bread in it; but she lacks for nothing in that way—heaps of money!

BARTOLOZZI.

Lucky woman! Give me bread before art. I've tried art on a lean stomach.

KAUFFMANN.

And it made you an artist, Bartolozzi!

1

BARTOLOZZI.

The stomach the seat of genius, hey? At any rate, it's a clever teacher, and a sharp master. But where's Angelica? I want a word with her.

KAUFFMANN.

Attending my Lady Margaret at Mr. Christie's sale-room—the last sale of the Chelsea china. They are inseparable. But she will be here directly to get on with her big picture "Arcadia,"

(Points to easel)

which is to compete for membership in this new Royal Academy they are all agog about.

BARTOLOZZI.

I'm in for the competition myself. Membership will be a great honour if the thing takes root and lives. I doubt it. Anything stirring with Angelica's love affairs?

KAUFFMANN.

Magnificent things! if I could only teach her to play the cards she holds.

(Angelica enters L.)

Between ourselves, two lovers at her feet.

ANGELICA.

Father, you must not talk in this way—nonsense!

KAUFFMANN.

Your settlement in life; it's my duty. I'm an old man —I cannot always be your protector.

BARTOLOZZI.

No secrets with your godfather. But, first of all, how are you, my child?

ANGELICA.

Quite well, dear Father Bartolozzi, if it wasn't for this endless bother about love. My father gives me no peace. Love is such a plague for a woman! Why do people love me? This man is nice, the other man is nice; they are all nice together, and there it ends. I'm sure I was made without a heart, or, at least, just enough to circulate the blood—that's all the use I can find for the thing people call a heart.

KAUFFMANN.

Count Strossman and Sir Joshua Reynolds for lovers! Something grand to choose from, if a woman has common wit.

BARTOLOZZI.

I've heard the rumour, and I've come with a caution. Not Count Strossman—it's playing with fire. I am told by the laws of Sweden that a nobleman cannot marry a commoner—it's no valid marriage.

KAUFFMANN.

Are you sure? Count Strossman! It would be such a splendid match for Angelica! My daughter a countess!

BARTOLOZZI.

Depend on it, my information is correct; so Count Strossman is out of the reckoning. But Sir Joshua remains—a great artist, and a title to boot.

KAUFFMANN.

Still, a painter's a painter; and Counts, with their ribbons and their stars——

ANGELICA.

Counts die, and there's an end of the stars. I admire and revere Sir Joshua—indeed, I do—but——

KAUFFMANN.

There's always a " but " in your love affairs. Look you, Bartolozzi—there's a certain young man that comes here—Count Strossman's valet—to sit as a model for the shepherd in the " Arcadia."

ANGELICA (with warmth).

Father! what do you mean?

KAUFFMANN.

Where there's a man you always contrive to flirt. It makes me half mad! He's a good-looking fellow; been brought up as a gentleman, they say—the illegitimate son of some great Swedish nobleman, that's the story.

ANGELICA.

Silence! Father, do you think for one moment that I should demean myself by giving the slightest encouragement to a person in such a position? I may pity him—I may pity a dog. Really, you must think your daughter a fool! A valet! Miss Angelica Kauffmann!—the valet of Count Strossman! It's a positive insult.

(In changed tones.)

There, father dear, I know your devotion to me from my earliest days. I will do all I can to please you. But Sir Joshua—I don't believe he really cares for me. Just a chat about art—rather animated sometimes—but, after all, only painting-room talk.

BARTOLOZZI.

Trust me, that's how love will begin with Sir Joshua. He's very shy with women—keeps them at a distance with his courtly manner; but art is his vulnerable point, Cupid's bull's-eye; that's the mark for your arrows, Angelica!

KAUFFMANN.

Ay, and the fear of a rival—if Count Strossman can't be a husband, he may serve as a rival.

BARTOLOZZI.

Curiously enough, I am the bearer of a commission from Count Strossman. They want a pictorial design for their invitation tickets for the big ball they are going to give at the Swedish Embassy. Mr. Cipriani was commissioned to send in a sketch, but Count Strossman don't like his work—too heavy in character—he directs me to offer you a commission—twenty pounds for a sketch—a liberal hand, indeed! Something you could knock off in two or three hours, light and bright—only he must have it this evening without fail; he is obliged to forward it to the Ambassador, who is staying at Bath for the waters, by early despatch to-morrow morning. Cipriani has wasted the time. I'm to engrave the plate. I love to work from your drawings, Angelica mine.

ANGELICA.

And sometimes correct the drawing. I shall be delighted. Twenty pounds would be very nice, wouldn't it, father, with all this furniture to buy for the new house? But I was going to see Dr. Goldsmith's new comedy this evening with Lady Margaret — " She Stoops to Conquer," that's the name, isn't it?

KAUFFMANN.

Take the twenty pounds, my child, and give up the comedy. If the comedy lives, you can see it another night; if it dies, as they say it will, you'll have been saved a dull evening.

ANGELICA.

I accept the commission, and give up the play. I can knock off the sketch by candle-light, and now I'll do a little work on the big picture—finish off my shepherd—or I shall be all behind-hand with " Arcadia."

(Rings bell.)

KAUFFMANN.

Now you are here, Bartolozzi, I want you to price some old drawings I picked up in Italy. I meant to sell 'em at Christie's. Say, Carlo Dolce—it's a good name just now to catch the buyers, though I prefer Raphael—but Count Strossman wants to buy them privately. They are in the library.

BARTOLOZZI.

Bravo, Mr. Count! He's a true patron of art! I'll price your Carlo Dolce's—or Carlo anythings you like—that will catch your connoisseurs. The Count can afford to pay a liberal price.

(Exeunt Bartolozzi and Kauffmann into library. Enter Servant.)

ANGELICA.

Tell Count Strossman's valet to wait on me.

(Exit Servant. Angelica goes to table, takes up palette, maulstick and brushes.)

A valet, indeed! To be accused of thinking for one moment of a valet! It is true he has much to endure, unfortunate young man; that his manners are those of a gentleman by birth and education—but a valet! If he were not a valet—— I am angry with myself. Perhaps I have been too condescending in my manner. There shall be no mistake from henceforth.

(Fersen enters.)

FERSEN (bows).

I am at your service, madam, your very humble servant.

ANGELICA (without noticing him, but intent on blending colours on the palette).

Take your seat, the same pose as yesterday.

(Fersen sits in attitude, Angelica looking up.)

No, no; you must hold the crook in your right hand—don't you remember?

(Takes up a gilt crook which is leaning against easel, and places it in Fersen's hand.)

Extend the right arm, as I told you.

(Returns to easel.)

That will do—head turned a little more to the right.

(Paints in silence.)

FERSEN.

Madam, what have I done?

ANGELICA.

Done? What should you do? You have attended, according to my directions.

FERSEN.

But your manner to-day is so different from yesterday —kind and gracious——

ANGELICA.

You interrupt my work; pray be silent !

FERSEN.

Silent ! and my fault unknown, and therefore un-atoned.

ANGELICA.

Fersen, it is not your place to address me—you forget yourself.

FERSEN.

I do; I have forgotten myself ever since I met you.

ANGELICA.

I forbid you to speak. If you will not be silent I must dismiss you. Presumption is most unbecoming in a person of your station.

FERSEN.

I pray your pity. Oh ! have a little mercy. Recollect the story of my life.

ANGELICA.

You have told it me more than once. I really have no time to lose in fruitless talk.

FERSEN.

Are these cold words from the heart that has felt so deeply for my misfortunes, that has encouraged me to tell the tale ? Think of it ! Brought up as befits the heir to a great title and estate; and then, at my father's death, my cruel relations discover that my poor mother was a commoner by birth—that her marriage, before men, was invalid. Cast out with ignominy—mother and son—into the hard world, without a home, without a name!

ANGELICA.

Once and again—you have told me all this, and I have pitied you—can I do more?

FERSEN.

I have told you the one dream, the one hope of my sad life—that the nobility of my mother's birth may yet be proved. There are good men, good lawyers, trying to help me in Sweden; Count Strossman even is trying to help me, in his harsh way—restoration to title and estate! That large hope to support me in my misery—and now I tell you that from henceforth I discard that hope.

ANGELICA.

What do you mean?

FERSEN.

Bear with me, in mercy! I am half mad! Your coldness drives me to frenzy. I say, I have discarded that hope.

ANGELICA.

Why?

FERSEN.

Because I love you. If I am restored to title and honour, we are separated for ever. I can never marry you.

ANGELICA.

Sir, you talk in a very wild and foolish manner! You dare to talk of love and marriage to me! Count Strossman's valet——

FERSEN.

I can fling off the plush!

ANGELICA.

Be reasonable. A beggar without a name!

FERSEN.

I can win a name, or die. The battlefield! The world's full of war—and then, fame and honour at your feet.

ANGELICA.

Discard such absurd thoughts; and, once more, be silent for your own sake, or I must end the sitting. Your master, Count Strossman, would be very angry.

FERSEN.

My master while I choose; but I am not his slave. I cannot be silent. Come what may, at least you shall know the truth. I love you—wildly, madly, hopelessly— but I love you!

ANGELICA.

Leave this room! Go, or I shall ring the bell!

(Goes towards bell.)

FERSEN.

And then they will drive me from this house. But this much you shall know, that somewhere in this world a heart lives for you alone; that love, honour, and reverence dwell in that heart—yours for ever—my gift to you—your possession; trample on it, if you will; scorn it, if you will —but yours for ever, till death's mercy ends the pain!

(Kauffmann enters.)

ANGELICA (with agitation).

Father—this young man—his language——

KAUFFMANN.

I overheard his insolence.

ANGELICA.

Let him go.

KAUFFMANN.

His master shall be told of this.

ANGELICA.

No; let him go, I say—I insist!

(Servant enters, announces "Count Strossman." Strossman enters, followed by Hans, bearing a bouquet.)

STROSSMAN (bowing to Angelica).

Good-day, fair lady ; but—some commotion, I fear ?

ANGELICA.

Nothing, Count. I was saying that I shall not require the presence of Fersen for any more sittings.

KAUFFMANN.

The Count shall know the truth. This young man has forgotten his position, and has dared to address unbecoming language to my daughter, which ought to be punished.

ANGELICA.

Not so ; a simple rebuke, if you will. As a particular favour, I request that no more notice may be taken of this trifling affair.

STROSSMAN.

At your desire, fair and gracious lady, no undue notice shall be taken.
(Calls.)
Fersen, my hat and cane.

FERSEN.

Count Strossman, I am no longer your valet.

STROSSMAN.

Unwise and hasty—you'll starve !

FERSEN.

There's bread in the world. I have hands and strength.

STROSSMAN.

True ; but your mother lives on my bounty—is she to starve ? Be wise ; you know me.
(Fersen irresolute.)
Take my hat and cane.
(Fersen, after a pause, comes forward and takes Strossman's hat and cane.)
Place them on that table ; then take that bouquet from

Hans, and present it to Miss Kauffmann with your master's devoted service.

(Fersen obeys.)

ANGELICA.

Spare him, I pray.

STROSSMAN

Pardon me, Miss Kauffmann, I must be allowed to have my own way with my own servants.—Present the bouquet.

FERSEN.

Madam, by my master's command I present this bouquet to you with his devoted service.

(Angelica takes bouquet with reluctance.)

STROSSMAN.

Pray this lady's pardon for your insolence.

ANGELICA.

It is nothing—I protest——

FERSEN.

Madam, I——

STROSSMAN.

On your knees—obey !

FERSEN (with intense effort submits and kneels).

Madam, I humbly pray your pardon.

ANGELICA (deeply agitated).

It is granted, freely granted.

(Staggers back, letting the bouquet fall from her hand.)

Father, I cannot bear this any longer—your arm.

(Takes Kauffmann's arm.)

Lady Margaret is waiting for me, I must go.

(Angelica and Kauffmann go out by library, he supporting her.)

STROSSMANN (motions to Fersen, who picks up bouquet. Aside).

So, my fair one loves this young man ; knowledge is always useful.

(Aloud to Fersen.)

You love this woman, do you ? Sir, your betters first !

Fool! have I never flung you my cast-off clothes? Attend, you have the list of the guests invited to my supper to-night: write a letter to each in my name, stating, with deep regret, that the supper is unavoidably postponed; give the letters to Hans, who will deliver them personally at the theatre. With the exception of the letters, everything else as previously ordered.

FERSEN.

The supper?

STROSSMAN.

Strictly according to orders—no change. I shall have one guest—one honoured guest. Go at once, and write the letters. By the way, the major-domo tells me he can't sleep o' nights. I've promised him a narcotic; let him have the bottle from my medicine-chest labelled "Sleep." Poor man! I think it will give him the repose he requires. Go!

FERSEN (aside).

One honoured guest! Drugged sleep, he means. Can it be possible—a plot against her honour?

STROSSMAN.

Why do you linger? Quickly with those letters.

FERSEN.

At once, your Excellency. The supper?

STROSSMAN.

I've said so; as ordered—no change. Go!

FERSEN (aside).

In his hands—Angelica alone—can it be? I will save her, if I die.

(Exit.)

STROSSMAN (to Hans).

When you have received the letters from Fersen, go to Covent Garden Theatre and deliver them during the performance. You know all the persons by sight; make no mistake, or you'll suffer for it. You are not to deliver the letter addressed to Miss Kauffmann; destroy it. When you have delivered the letters at the theatre, come on here with my coach. Miss Kauffmann will be ready. When she is safely in the carriage, drive post-haste to Chelsea. Don't fail; be secret and discreet. Above all, not one word to Fersen; he can't be trusted in this delicate affair. Some day, I shall make you my valet in his place.

(Hans bows and goes out.)

To win a woman, is it worth all this trouble? Why, I might win a diplomatic triumph, outwit cunning ambassadors with less labour; the process is magnificent, but the result is very small. A straight path to fame and honour, and yet I madly turn aside and pursue a butterfly —crushed in the hand that grasps it, and then cast away —a residuum of tears, remorse—the cold ashes of passion —nothing better to show for a triumph. Pooh! logic to cure madness! It's all in vain; mine she must be!

(Lady Margaret enters.)

Ah, my Lady Margaret, how fares the grand passion?

LADY MARGARET.

Ill, Count.

STROSSMAN.

Sir Joshua is constantly at your house.

LADY MARGARET.

Angelica is the attraction.

STROSSMAN.

That's your opportunity! Turn the attraction to your-self.

LADY MARGARET.

Sir Joshua is absorbed in his love of art.

STROSSMAN.

But you are a lady of noble birth, and she is only fit to be your waiting-woman.

LADY MARGARET.

An artist !

STROSSMAN.

What is an artist in comparison with a grand lady ?
I'm sick of this cant about the nobility of art !

LADY MARGARET.

But you love her—you say you love her !

STROSSMAN.

Love her ? Yes ; love her !

LADY MARGARET.

But you cannot marry her.

STROSSMAN.

Marry her ! Our law in Sweden forbids the marriage
of a noble with a commoner. But, in any event, do you
suppose I should stoop to marry a plebeian? Honour
enough for her that I choose to love her—to honour her
with my love.

LADY MARGARET.

But Sir Joshua ? You know my secret, for you yourself have guessed it. I love that man—I would gladly
marry him, but this woman stands between me and my
desperate hope. I entertain her in this house because she
serves to bring him here ; but I suffer an agony when he
comes. Sometimes I think it were better to send her
away and end it all—the pain is too great !

STROSSMAN.

What was my pledge ?

LADY MARGARET.

That she should never marry Sir Joshua, because you
love her—always that string.

STROSSMAN.

I possess another string, which the fortune of to-day has discovered. Take comfort, two strings! Come what may, I say she shall never marry Sir Joshua Reynolds.

(Angelica enters from library. Strossman addresses her with gallant air.)

Fair lady, a thousand apologies for that painful scene.

ANGELICA.

Let it all pass, I pray you; and let me thank you for that liberal commission—far too liberal for the work required.

STROSSMAN.

And you will execute it this evening?

ANGELICA.

Certainly; to the best of my power.

STROSSMAN.

It's a whim of mine. I want to show your work to my guests to-night. They shall decide between you and Mr. Cipriani. I wager the victory will be yours; and then I must send it off by earliest despatch to Bath for his Excellency's inspection. We are all impatient for the invitations to be issued for the grand ball. It will be magnificent! All the Court, all the *élite* of society, will be present —and Miss Kauffmann, if she will deign to honour his Excellency with her presence?

ANGELICA.

Count, you are too gracious—a humble artist, almost a stranger in England.

STROSSMAN.

I protest, madam, the honour will be ours. There is no honour too great for Miss Kauffmann. When his Excellency returns to town, I promise you all his patronage and favour. All my poor influence in society is already yours. The commissions will flock in.

ANGELICA.

A thousand thanks for all this unmerited kindness !

STROSSMAN.

Nay, madam ; Genius commands, I only obey.   There were some drawings by the Old Masters which your good father promised should be mine.

(Kauffmann enters from library.)

Ah ! Mr. Kauffmann, those drawings — I have your promise.

KAUFFMANN.

They are yours, Count, at your service.   My friend, Mr. Bartolozzi, has just valued them.   He names a large sum, I confess—one hundred pounds !

STROSSMAN.

They are mine.   Prompt payment is my maxim.

KAUFFMANN.

Nay, Count——

STROSSMAN.

I have the money, I think.

(Takes out notes, which he gives to Kauffmann.)

And now, fair lady, if you will graciously accept at my hands the value of your commission.

(Gives note to Angelica.)

ANGELICA (starts).

Why—why—— I have no change ! It's a note for fifty pounds !

(Offers to return note.)

Twenty was the sum, and that was too liberal by far.

STROSSMAN.

Pardon me, that was Mr. Bartolozzi's estimate ; my estimate exceeds his.

ANGELICA.

Father, what must I do ?   This is robbery !

KAUFFMANN.

Commit the crime, my child, and thank his Excellency for his generous patronage.

ANGELICA.

It shall be my best work, that's all I can say.

STROSSMAN.

And you will bring it this evening to my supper, where you will reign as queen, crowned with your own laurels. I can promise you the devotion of one loyal subject—your very devoted and humble servant.

(Bows. Servant enters and announces "Miss Reynolds, my lady." Miss Reynolds enters, Servant goes out.)

MISS REYNOLDS.

Lady Margaret, your most obedient. Angelica—Count Strossman.

(Bows stiffly to the Count.)

Lady Margaret, I have come on a double mission. Joshua is finishing off a sitting as long as the light lasts, and then he'll follow me. First, business—I manage all my brother's business arrangements. I have to request you, Lady Margaret, to put off your sitting for to-morrow morning, as Joshua has received a command to attend his Majesty on the affairs of the new Academy. My next mission is pleasure. Joshua has secured one of the best boxes to-night at Covent Garden for Dr. Goldsmith's comedy; he requests Lady Margaret and Miss Kauffmann to share the box with us. We can all go together, and afterwards go to Count Strossman's supper in Joshua's coach.

LADY MARGARET.

I shall be delighted. Sir Joshua is too good to honour us in this way!

MISS REYNOLDS.

My lady, the honour is his. And you, Angelica?

2

STROSSMAN.

I am afraid I must interpose, with deep regret; but
Miss Kauffmann has promised to devote the evening to me
—the design for our ball tickets, which is urgent.

ANGELICA.

I have given my promise to the Count; but I shall join
you all at supper.

STROSSMAN.

My coach will convey Miss Kauffmann safely to Cheyne
Walk. I only regret that I should be an obstacle to this
evening's amusement; but, after all, the amusement seems
doubtful.

MISS REYNOLDS.

A comedy by Dr. Goldsmith?

STROSSMAN.

I hear, on the best authority, that Manager Colman is
in despair; that he has been driven to produce the play
against his own judgment; that all the best actors, Mrs.
Abingdon to boot, have thrown up their parts—and actors
ought to know what a play is. A most absurd plot!
Just fancy a man in his seven senses mistaking a gentleman's country house for a country inn! The idea is too
absurd for a farce—and what person of refined taste could
tolerate a farce which is to last a whole evening? We
have not come to that yet, thank the gods!

MISS REYNOLDS.

Dr. Johnson thinks the play an excellent comedy.

STROSSMAN.

Madam, three or four hours will decide between the
learned doctor and your very unlearned servant.
(Bows.)
But, unless I'm a fool, "She Stoops to Conquer" will go
out like a damp squib, and be heard of no more in the

history of the drama. And now, ladies, duties of State call me away from this delightful society, your most obedient—— Au revoir, till to-night, when I shall have the honour of playing the host to you in my own *inn* at Cheyne Walk, Chelsea.

(Bows.)

KAUFFMANN.

Count, grant the favour of a few minutes to inspect the drawings which you have purchased.

STROSSMAN.

Certainly, if Miss Kauffmann will be good enough to point out their beauties.

KAUFFMANN.

My daughter will be delighted. In the library, Count. Angelica, my child, show the Count.

(Angelica goes out to library followed by Strossman and Kauffmann.)

MISS REYNOLDS.

I hate that man !

LADY MARGARET.

Dear madam, I protest. A man of fashion, and a man of taste !

MISS REYNOLDS.

I hate him because he is always paying attentions to Angelica.

LADY MARGARET.

Her attractions and her talent.

MISS REYNOLDS.

He has no right to trifle with her, because he can never marry her—that's the law of his country. Now, once more to business. I never had such business on hand before. My lady, you must give me all the help you can ; my brother is in love with Angelica—the first woman he has ever cared for—and I'm at a nonplus.

LADY MARGARET.

What's the difficulty ?

MISS REYNOLDS.

Women always frighten him.

LADY MARGARET.

But he is always so gallant to ladies—compliments, and delightful flatteries.

MISS REYNOLDS.

That's from fright. It keeps them off. Gallantry is his shield—flattery, a coat-of-mail, and behind the armour, sheer fright. But he's in love now—dying to make an offer, and he doesn't know the way. You see, women have always existed in his mind as ideals, not human beings— so many yards of painted canvas, light and shade, drapery, schemes of colour, bankers' cheques even, but not flesh and blood. " Law! Joshua," I tell him, " talk to her anyhow." But that's the rub ; "anyhow" blocks the way. If I could only make Angelica understand—just a little help over the stones. Couldn't you help us by giving her a hint—just a wee, tiny hint—very indirect, of course ; I mean a sort of something round the corner ?

LADY MARGARET.

My dear madam, impossible ! I could not interfere in such a delicate affair. I must be pardoned. You must excuse me while I change my dress for the theatre ; it's getting late.

(Aside.)

I must let Count Strossman know that matters are imminent, if he wants to secure Angelica.

(Exit.)

MISS REYNOLDS.

If Lady Margaret won't help, I must tell her myself. It's very awkward—something round the corner always is

awkward—but it will be still more awkward if the offer is
never made.

(Angelica enters from library.)

Well, I hope you detest that odious Count Strossman—
I do!

ANGELICA.

Indeed, Miss Reynolds, you don't do him justice! He
is vastly gracious and considerate—most liberal in his
patronage both to my father and myself.

MISS REYNOLDS.

A nobleman, granted; but, recollect, he can never
marry you!

ANGELICA.

The idea of marriage never entered into my head!

MISS REYNOLDS.

Well, but there are other people who *can* marry you—
there are other people who would like to marry you—
there are other people's sisters who would like you to
marry them.

(Aside.)

I hope that's as clear as the best logic.

ANGELICA.

Several husbands, madam? And all the sisters?

MISS REYNOLDS.

No; *one* husband, if you are not a goose—saving your
presence—and one sister-in-law.

ANGELICA.

Madam, I protest.

MISS REYNOLDS.

That's just what you mustn't do. You must assent
before you are asked, or you never will be asked. You
must keep "Yes" ready to jump out of your mouth, like
a Jack-in-the-box—the slightest touch, snap goes the

spring, and, presto! there stands "Yes" smiling and
smirking on your lips.   Mark my words, a nimble "Yes"
will make you a lady of title, with a fine house, before
you know where you are; a lazy "Yes," and you may die
a spinster!

(Aside.)

It's round the corner, but I think I've made it plain
enough.

(Sir Joshua enters.)

Why, here's Joshua come to take us to the theatre. Lady
Margaret is beautifying herself before the glass; Miss
Kauffmann can't go because she has a commission to
execute for Count Strossman. I'll tell Lady Margaret
that you are here;

(Aside to Sir Joshua)

and keep her employed. Out with it, Joshua, or Count
Strossman will carry her off under your very nose, and
then you'll be sorry in vain. Why, it's so easy; four
little letters spell "love"—short, and very sweet.

(Exit.)

SIR JOSHUA (with embarrassment).

Madam, I must express my profound regret that you
are unable to accompany us to the theatre.

ANGELICA.

I deeply regret it also; but the claims of Art are sacred.
You will forgive me for yielding to their demands?

SIR JOSHUA.

Assuredly, my dear lady. To an artist, art must be the
one object of life—emphatically the sole object of exist-
ence.

ANGELICA.

I feel that.

SIR JOSHUA.

With fervour?

ANGELICA.

With my whole heart.

SIR JOSHUA (with warmth).

That is the spirit I love to behold in the artist!—the spirit that leads through hard toil to fame. And you, a woman, with all woman's charms, are positively prepared to forget woman's fascination for the sake of art; to forego her triumphs in the world, in society; to declare yourself the votary of art—the painting-room a cloister, secluded from all other thoughts—the devotion of a nun to holy vows.

ANGELICA.

A nun!

SIR JOSHUA.

My dear lady, the fervent artist should, above all things, avoid the distractions of the heart. Well enough for other women, but fatal snares for the artist; the common cares of life quickly invade the soul, and drive out the nobler thoughts. Let other women marry if they will—the artist should never marry! Tell me that you have forsworn all weakness of the affections.

ANGELICA.

I have, Sir-Joshua; I have cast away all such folly; I live for art alone.

SIR JOSHUA.

Let me grasp your hand on that assurance.
    (Holds her hand.)
It clears away all obstacles from the path of fame.
    (With fervour.)
My heart beats with yours! We are animated by one common feeling, you and I. We are content to live for nothing but our noble profession—sympathetic bond—sister, brother—in this common link.

ANGELICA.

Sister, if you so honour me; but pupil rather. Teach me; I am very humble in the sense of my own deficiency. Oh! that it might be my privilege to watch the growth of

your great works—the untouched canvas, already aglow
in your mind's eye with glorious purpose—the gradual
progress from the first brush touch to the crowning
triumph !

SIR JOSHUA.

Ah, Miss Angel, your presence would be perpetual
inspiration—sunlight to my soul. I feel assured that the
sacred flame burns in our hearts! I can refrain no
longer; I will confess the new secret which fills my heart
with joy.

ANGELICA (aside).

A confession at last.

SIR JOSHUA.

Listen, you shall know all. Spirit of turpentine——

ANGELICA.

Turpentine !

SIR JOSHUA.

Heated to boiling-point, pure white wax; boil together
for ten minutes — that's all.

ANGELICA.

All ?

SIR JOSHUA.

Delicious vehicle ! The very thought of it fills the soul
with delight.

ANGELICA (aside).

Varnish and the soul !

(Aloud.)

The very compound I have been seeking in vain. My
poor " Arcadia " looks so dull and dark.

SIR JOSHUA.

Let us see. You are always so modest with regard to
your own work. I love modesty in an artist; diffidence
is always pleasing.

(They go up to canvas.)

Excellent progress ! Charming sentiment, and colour very
pleasant ; a little glazing in due course.

ANGELICA.

But full of errors, alas!

SIR JOSHUA.

Not so—not so. Ay—one moment. The drawing of that arm—something amiss. I'll show you. A bit of chalk.

(Angelica offers chalk to Sir Joshua)

No; you take it. I want you to make the alteration. You see what I mean?

ANGELICA.

I can't, indeed; I'm——

SIR JOSHUA.

I'll guide your hand.

(Takes her hand in his.)

Just so. Why, how your hand trembles—my arm—your whole frame trembles! Oh! Miss Kauffmann—Angel— if it were only mine to guide you—to guide you always! Tell me, could you be content with my guidance in art?

ANGELICA.

Content? No; happy—proud, and very happy.

(Stones are thrown at window, she starts away, listening intently.)

SIR JOSHUA.

Eh? What's that?

FERSEN (outside).

Miss Kauffmann! Miss Kauffmann!

SIR JOSHUA.

A man's voice!

ANGELICA.

This is too scandalous and shameful!

(Lady Margaret enters R., Kauffmann enters L.)

LADY MARGARET.

What is that noise outside? Thieves at this hour—impossible!

ANGELICA.

Not thieves, Lady Margaret; it is only Count Strossman's impertinent valet.

LADY MARGARET (with concealed exultation).

What, that handsome young man who has been sitting to you as a model for " Arcadia "? A model turned into a lover !—but you attract everybody.

ANGELICA.

Nonsense, Lady Margaret ! The insolent fellow has been forbidden the house at my desire, but he still dares to persecute me in this odious way—insanity, I suppose.

LADY MARGARET.

The insanity of love !

KAUFFMANN.

Mad or sane, the cur shall be whipped off the premises. Where are the servants ?

ANGELICA.

No, father; let him say what he has to say. There must be no concealment ; my reputation demands a public vindication.

(Goes to window and throws it open, Fersen is discovered crouched down on his knees.)

Come in, sir, since you have dared to seek my presence in this unwarrantable manner !

(Fersen rises and enters ; he is dazed at the presence of the other persons.)

FERSEN (to Angelica).

Lady, for Heaven's sake, a word to you in private !

ANGELICA.

In private ! No ; speak out, sir ! Why did you venture here ? You have been already turned out of the house on account of your impertinence.

FERSEN.

I dare not speak openly; I can only speak to you alone.

ANGELICA.

I say, you shall speak openly—I am compromised by your conduct.

FERSEN (in low tone to Angelica).

I came to save you.

ANGELICA (repeating in loud tone).

You came to save me? What do you mean? Speak plainly, I say.

FERSEN (in low tone).

Do not go to Count Strossman's supper.

ANGELICA (in loud tone).

"Do not go to Count Strossman's supper!" Are you mad? Why not? Everyone is going—a large party of my friends—all the world! Your words are absurd.

FERSEN.

Do not go, I beg and pray; nay, listen to me. For mercy's sake! if you only knew——

ANGELICA.

Silence, sir! not one word more! This is some senseless excuse framed for the moment. You know you came here to persecute me with your ridiculous suit—you, a valet! For this insolent folly, I have already prayed your pardon from Count Strossman. I was wrong; the Count shall be informed of this new impertinence. Go, sir, at once!

KAUFFMANN.

At once, you insolent scoundrel!

(Snatches up maulstick, and rushes on Fersen.)

ANGELICA (trying to restrain her father).

Father, no violence!

Kauffmann strikes Fersen. With a burst of indignation, Fersen wrests the stick from Kauffmann, who retires back, half-drawing his sword. Fersen breaks the stick across his knee, restrains himself, and drops the two pieces gently at the feet of Angelica.)

FERSEN.

Oh, Miss Kauffmann, may you never have cause to repent that blow! Mad—yes, mad!

(Hurries out of the room by door C.)

KAUFFMANN (to Sir Joshua).

Sir Joshua, I trust—the conduct of this insolent menial—my daughter's reputation risked in this wanton way by a madman——

SIR JOSHUA (coldly).

Sir, Miss Kauffmann's honour requires no vindication in such a contemptible matter.

(To Lady Margaret.)

My Lady Margaret, it must be time to start for the theatre.

(Offers his arm to Lady Margaret.)

LADY MARGARET.

Miss Reynolds is waiting for us in the drawing-room.

SIR JOSHUA (bowing with ceremony to Angelica.)

Miss Kauffmann, I have the honour to wish you good-evening.

(Sir Joshua leads out Lady Margaret in stately manner, Angelica and her father watch their exit in silence.)

KAUFFMANN.

My child, but for that scoundrel, "Lady Reynolds"!

ANGELICA.

Nay, your daughter—happiness enough for Angelica.

(She throws herself into his arms.

CURTAIN.

ACT II.

COUNT DE HORNE.

SCENE.

Ante-room in Count Strossman's mansion at Chelsea. C., large entrance with double doors from a corridor leading from the hall of the house. R. (2nd entrance) large entrance with double doors to supper-room. L. (2nd entrance) corresponding entrance to drawing-room. L. (1st entrance) panel door, being a secret entrance from garden. The whole scene is brilliantly lighted for the reception of guests. On each side of centre entrance are handsome girandoles with lights and long cut-glass pendant spikes and balls. Table R., settee L. The room is handsomely furnished in the style of the period. On rise of curtain, two men-servants and two women-servants are discovered dressed in rich costumes as mock guests; they are talking and laughing, and displaying their clothes. Strossman enters R.; the servants stand before him in attitudes of constraint.

STROSSMAN (surveys them).

Excellent, I declare. I scarcely recognise you as my servants. Bear yourselves a little more easily, and you'll pass for persons of distinction; a clever dash of imitation and the outer garb, why, you might be all of noble birth.

(Aside.)

Ay, menials at soul, and yet dress and manners serve as often as not for a disguise in the world of fashion.

(Aloud.)

Now, my mock guests, attend to my instructions. When my fair guest arrives, echo all my words of admiration, praise when I praise, laugh when I laugh, follow my moods as they vary. Remember, the highest expression of honour and respect to Miss Kauffmann is the keynote

of your conduct.   Play your parts well; you know I have
a liberal hand.

(Hans enters booted and spurred.)

Ah, Hans! have you delivered the letters, postponing the
supper, to all the invited guests at the theatre ?

HANS.

Yes, Count.

STROSSMAN.

Everybody ?—are you sure?   It would destroy my
scheme if any one of them turned up.

HANS.

Everybody.

STROSSMAN.

And Miss Kauffmann ?

HANS.

Safely on the road.   As soon as I had placed her in
your coach, I galloped forward to prepare you for her
arrival.

STROSSMAN.

Admirable !   To-morrow, count on your reward.

HANS.

More than this, Count, I intercepted a letter just
written by Fersen to Miss Kauffmann; I thought it might
mean mischief.

(Gives letter to Strossman, which he opens and reads.)

STROSSMAN.

It does mean mischief—a warning in plain terms, dis-
closing the whole story of my design !   Curse the fellow !
He dares to stand between me and my purpose !   The
fool ! he shall rue his folly before we part.   Where is
Fersen ?

HANS.

In the audience-chamber, waiting your Excellency's orders.

STROSSMAN.

Hans, one word.

(Whispers to Hans.)

Fersen may be dangerous; he must be made sure of for to-night; to-morrow he shall be shipped off under hatches to Sweden. Let him be secured in the tower chamber; he'll be safe there.

HANS.

The secret records, your Excellency?

STROSSMAN.

They are under lock and key. He can do no harm. Go to him at once; say I require the last despatch from Stockholm. Here is the key of the door;

(Gives key)

open the door for him, and when he enters the room, turn the key quickly—he'll sleep comfortably till morning.

(Loud knock at hall door.)

Ah, the fair artist comes! You know my directions. Have you the phial ready, and the wine?

(Hans shows phial.)

Now, be quick, and place Fersen under lock and key.

(Voice of servant in hall: Miss Angelica Kauffman!)

Victory of love! in another minute she will be safely in my power!

(Voice in corridor: Miss Angelica Kauffmann!)

(The folding doors C. are flung open; Angelica appears in doorway, the mock guests arise and bow; Angelica curtsies at entrance, Strossman advances towards her. Fersen suddenly appears in doorway and tries to stop Angelica's entrance.)

FERSEN (to Angelica).

Do not enter! You are lost! My letter!—you had my letter an hour ago?

ANGELICA (with indignation to Fersen).

Leave me, sir !   Your conduct becomes unbearable.
(She advances with indignation to Strossman.)
Count Strossman, I am obliged at last seriously to invoke
your interference.   This young man's conduct is most
scandalous !   This is the third time to-day that I have had
to submit to his insolent behaviour !

FERSEN.

Hear me, for Heaven's sake, or you are lost !

STROSSMAN.

Silence, sir !   Ho, there !
(Two servants stand in doorway.)

ANGELICA.

Count, I ask for your protection; my character is
actually compromised by this man's persistence; he has
no right to address me in such a manner.

STROSSMAN (to Fersen).

You hear, sir—leave this room !

FERSEN.

Not while Miss Kauffmann remains here.

STROSSMAN (sharply to Hans).

Fool !   Deal with him—no delay.
(Hans and the two men seize Fersen, and drag him struggling towards
the door.)
FERSEN (speaking with difficulty).

Miss Kauffmann, I tell you, you are in danger—shame
—disgrace !
STROSSMAN.

Stop the cursed fellow's tongue !
(Hans forces handkerchief into Fersen's mouth, and he is dragged
out by Hans and servants. The foldii g-doors are closed after
them.)
An insolent cur !   A young man I have befriended in his

misfortunes.   Madness !   His head must be turned—that's the only explanation for such wild folly.

(To Angelica.)

Dear madam, a thousand apologies for this untoward reception.   I promise you that Fersen will not annoy you any more by his presence this evening ; to-morrow he will be shipped off to Sweden.   And now, permit me to introduce you to these good friends of mine, who are here to do honour to your artistic fame.   Ladies and gentlemen, Miss Angelica Kauffmann, the renowned artist.   Count Rupert and the Countess of Stralsound ; Count Borgen ; the Countess Gerssen.

(They all bow with great ceremony to Angelica, who duly acknowledges their salutations.)

And now, fair lady, you must let me tell you that these guests of mine are great connoisseurs in art ; and I need not say that we are all impatience to see the sketch you so graciously promised to execute for my gratification this evening.

ANGELICA.

I have it here, Count, according to my promise; but I am afraid it is unworthy of your liberality.   If you could have granted me a little longer time——

(Gives sketch to Strossman, who examines it intently.)

STROSSMAN.

Most lovely !   Look, ladies and gentlemen !

(Mock guests gather round Strossman.)

Bright, charming fancy !   A dance of nymphs and satyrs, with old Pan and his pipes for music, and a whole chorus of delicious little Cupids in the clouds !   Delightful invention and charming execution !   And now I pray you to compare Miss Kauffmann's design with the design which Mr. Cipriani has furnished.

(Takes up a sketch from table, and holds the two sketches together for inspection.)

To my thinking, there is no comparison : the one is full of

graceful feeling, light and bright in conception ; the other
is laboured in design, and heavy in execution. Ladies
and gentlemen, I may be a partial judge—no one can be
impartial who has the honour of knowing Miss Kauffmann
—it shall be for your unbiased judgment to decide which
sketch bears the palm. Mr. Cipriani or Miss Kauffmann?
—give your verdict.

MOCK GUESTS.

Miss Kauffmann! Miss Kauffmann!

STROSSMAN.

There's the award ; you have won, fair artist, as I knew
you would. Ho! there. The wine of triumph. You
must know, fair lady, that it is our Swedish custom to
pledge the victor in all contests.

(Hans enters bearing a silver jug, followed by a servant with six
glasses on a salver.)

Fill it to the brim. The fullest measure is the measure of
our admiration for a great artist.

(Hans fills the glasses, which servant hands to mock guests and Strossman.)

ANGELICA.

But your other friends, Count—Sir Joshua, Dr. Johnson—who will be here directly? They may prefer Mr.
Cipriani's more solid work to my light fancies.

STROSSMAN.

They will never reverse the voice of Sweden. Fair
artist, Sweden drinks to your triumph. Miss Angelica
Kauffmann!

(Strossman and mock guests drink.)

OMNES.

Miss Kauffmann and her victory !

(Hans takes salver with remaining glass from servant, and in sight of
the audience pours phial into glass, which he offers on bended knee
to Angelica.)

ANGELICA.

No, I thank you, pray pardon me; I will not drink now. I scarcely ever touch wine.

STROSSMAN.

Our national custom, fair lady. You must graciously honour us by acknowledging our pledge.

ANGELICA.

If you insist, it would be churlish to refuse. My humble thanks for your gracious compliments and honour ; would they were better deserved !

(Drinks small portion of the wine.)

STROSSMAN.

A full draught, fair artist, is the measure of your acknowledgment.

ANGELICA.

Be it so; my lips shall not belie my heart.

(Drinks off wine.)

STROSSMAN.

A thousand thanks to you for so graciously honouring the customs of old Sweden.

ANGELICA.

What a charming house you possess, Count Strossman ! Everything around us testifies to your love of art.

STROSSMAN.

My house and all its contents are ever at Miss Kauffmann's disposal.

ANGELICA.

You are far too gracious !

STROSSMAN.

Ah, fair lady, I have many bright things to please bright eyes. You must see my diamonds—the family jewels— set in our old northern setting—lovely goldwork ! You

shall choose what you like in honour of this happy evening
and your artistic triumph.

ANGELICA.

I could not, indeed; you have already doubly paid me
for my poor work. But our friends, what can have
detained them? Surely the play must be over by this
time.

STROSSMAN.

What friends, fair lady?

ANGELICA.

The friends invited to your supper.

STROSSMAN.

I have only one friend who has been gracious enough to
honour me with her presence.

ANGELICA.

But they are coming—Sir Joshua and his sister, Lady
Margaret, Dr. Johnson, Mr. Bartolozzi, Mr. Boswell, and
a large party?

STROSSMAN.

Fair lady, I repeat, *you* are my only guest.

ANGELICA.

But they were invited—they are coming, are they not?

STROSSMAN.

In your special honour, I have put off receiving those
worthy persons—we sup together.

ANGELICA.

What do you mean?

STROSSMAN.

Have you not long ago guessed my meaning? Have
you not felt that I loved you?

ANGELICA.

Loved me!

STROSSMAN.

Deeply, passionately, devotedly.

ANGELICA.

No, no; this is some jest, some ill-timed jest!

STROSSMAN.

No jest, on my honour—your devoted lover. Can you have been so blind?

ANGELICA.

Let me go—this moment, I say. It is a disgrace to remain in this house!

STROSSMAN.

Angelica, my sweet love, be reasonable. You know I cannot offer you marriage—the law of Sweden is inexorable, it forbids the marriage of a nobleman and a commoner. You cannot be my wife; but have no fear, there will be no scandal in my love: my guest for a few hours, and then you will return home in safety—only be discreet, and the world will never know the story of my happiness.

ANGELICA.

My shame! Villain! scoundrel! It was true, then—that devoted young man, whose warning I derided in my foolish faith and innocence. Let me go, I say, or I will denounce you in the presence of these ladies and gentlemen.

STROSSMAN.

My servants—my creatures, dressed up in your honour.

ANGELICA.

Impossible! Your servants! Is your villainy as deep as this? Servants—yes; but women—men—with human hearts.

(Going towards mock guests.)

Women, I appeal to you as a woman; save me—protect

me from that man, I pray—I pray! Think if I were your
sister—disgrace, shame, horror !

STROSSMAN.

Servants, leave the room.

(Angelica tries to cling to the women, but they put her away and leave
the room ; she clings to one of the men.)

ANGELICA.

Men, as you are men—a woman, I beg and pray for
protection. Do not leave me—do not leave me helpless in
that man's hands !

STROSSMAN (to men).

Leave the room, I say !

(The two men thrust Angelica aside and leave the room.)

Close the doors.

(The doors are all closed.)

ANGELICA.

No, no; have mercy ! Let me go. This is some cruel
trick to try me.

STROSSMAN.

Angelica, sweetest woman,

(Approaches her)

we are alone. Why so coy ?

ANGELICA.

Do not come near me, I am dangerous ! I have strength
enough to tear you in pieces ! Heaven will give me ten-
fold strength.

STROSSMAN.

Nay, sweet one, fear no violence ; I abhor violence. I
shall not win you with violence. I am a gentleman, not
a vulgar ruffian.

ANGELICA.

Then let me go.

STROSSMAN.

You shall go ; I promise that.

ANGELICA.

Now—at once!

STROSSMAN.

Impossible. If you left now, you would arrive home insensible with sleep.

ANGELICA.

Sleep! What do you mean?

STROSSMAN.

A soothing draught——

ANGELICA.

That wine!

STROSSMAN.

A harmless sedative. The effect will quickly pass away. An hour's sleep—quiet, unconscious sleep.

ANGELICA.

That accursed wine! That hellish draught! Villain! inhuman monster!

(In changed tone, casting herself at his feet.)

No, no; have mercy! You must have mercy. Before Heaven, I claim mercy. A miserable triumph—a woman, helpless, senseless, dead with sleep, unconscious, a victim to shame, disgrace! No man could do this. The triumph of a fiend, not a man! Such things cannot be in God's world.

(Sinks down exhausted.)

STROSSMAN.

You are unduly excited; sleep awhile, fairest lady— quiet sleep, that's all. I will leave you now. This is an inner room. Your voice cannot travel beyond these walls, so noise is useless. Sleep is inevitable—gentle, soothing, lulling sleep!

(Exit R.)

ANGELICA (raising her head and gazing round).

Sleep! sleep! Alone—but he will return. Oh, horror! trapped, vilely trapped! There must be some escape, some mercy.

(Rises and flies to centre door and knocks.)

I will give gold—gold to anyone who will save me; gold —what you will. No answer—no answer; all's in vain. No; that other door!

(Goes to door L. ; knocks.)

Save me! I will give you gold—all—everything I possess —only save me—a woman—a woman's honour! Mercy! mercy! No answer—no hope!

(Goes back to settee, flings herself upon it, clasping her hands over her face, then rises with look of despair.)

Impossible! it cannot he. But sleep!—he said sleep! Sleep will deliver me, a helpless victim, into his accursed arms! Oh, cruel sleep which wakes to shame! Is sleep stealing on me—the eyelids heavy? Not yet; but it will come. The accursed wine will work its vile purpose, coursing through the veins, dulling the healthy beatings of the heart; and then the horrible sleep will come—slowly, very slowly, like a mist creeping over brain and eyes, stealing away every sense, even the burning sense of shame! And then?—oh, Heaven, senseless—helpless— no escape! What help? No help! Only two things remain—dishonour or death. Death—be it death! How? how? Death somehow. How to seek death—some weapon! What weapon?

(Steals round the room seeking intently.)

No knife, no weapon, no help to death! Oh, Heaven, grant me this mercy, that I may escape the horror of that shame. Nothing—nothing to rid me of life, and the brain grows dull—sleep will come before I can find death! Death will be too late to save me.

(A pause ; then, suddenly looking round :)

Saved! saved!

(Flies to girandole, breaks off one of the spikes of glass, feels the splintered point.)

Sharp, like a lancet. Saved! Thank Heaven, I can die!

(Staggers back to settee and sits, placing fragment of glass by her side.)

Lie there, close at hand, and when I feel the mist rising in my brain, why, then—then—quick, to my heart! So easy; one inch to reach this beating thing of life, and then it stops—death—ay, stops for ever. But, strength for the blow—have I strength? My hand trembles!

(Cries.)

I am only a woman. And life—my father, my poor father, alone in the world; and ambition—to die now—now that I know what my hands can do, my brain invent—fame, honours, praise, flattery. Life's very sweet, and now the full cup of success is at my lips, and death to dash it down! I shall never have the strength for the blow. I cannot die—I cannot die! Life—I must have life, not cold, pulseless death—breathing, beating, burning life. I cannot die!

(Clasps her hands in despair over her face. Noise at panel door; Angelica starts up, and seizes the glass splinter.)

Who's there?

(Fersen enters.)

Approach one step, and I kill myself before your eyes. I can die—death, not shame. A sharp splinter of glass, and I die at your feet.

FERSEN (in low tone).

Hush! a friend. But silence, for Heaven's sake!

ANGELICA (perceiving Fersen).

You! What you!—you! Heaven's mercy!

(Flies to him, and clings convulsively to him.)

You will save me. They have given me drugged wine. When the horrible sleep comes, watch me, guard me—stand at my side—save my honour. Helpless, senseless; but in your arms I shall be safe.

FERSEN.

Softly, softly; we shall be heard, and then they will tear you from me. Sleep will not come.

ANGELICA.

But the wine?

FERSEN.

I changed the vile drug, and replaced it by some harmless mixture. Be assured, they cannot steal your senses.

ANGELICA.

My protector! my guardian! But how did you get into this room?

FERSEN.

I was locked into a tower chamber. I descended by the ivy.

ANGELICA.

At the danger of your life! Oh, brave and generous! On my knees—

(Kneels at his feet)

I thank you—poor words!—for a great devotion. You have saved me from a fate worse than death—saved me from the horror of a polluted life; and in my ignorance and my pride I have treated you with contempt and scorn —my father, myself—and yours was the true, noble heart which risked all for my sake, in despite of outrage, and insult, and cruel blows! What reward? what reward?

FERSEN (raising her).

Oh, Angel, pure and noble, my highest reward is to serve you, to save you from dishonour and shame. A wide gulf between us, but always the idol of my heart to reverence and worship!

ANGELICA.

Too generous! too noble! I am a poor debtor for a priceless gift. But, say, can we fly from this horrible place?—the way you entered?

FERSEN.

Impossible! the house is surrounded by Strossman's eople. I have devised a better plan: a little patience, a little more endurance, and all danger will be at an end, all scandal will be averted—you will leave this house as you have entered it, without reproach.

(Strossman enters R.)

STROSSMAN.

Scoundrel! you have dared to return!

FERSEN.

Scoundrel in your teeth! Approach this lady, and you die.

STROSSMAN (calls).

Ho! there—servants!

ANGELICA (to Fersen).

Do not leave me; I am very weak, all nerve has gone; and that vile wretch, with horrible purpose in his eyes— the fascination of a snake! Save me! save me!

(Two servants and Hans stand in door R.)

FERSEN.

Keep heart, dear lady; I will die ere they injure you.

STROSSMAN.

Secure that fellow quickly!

FERSEN (draws).

At your peril, men; you know my skill at fence.

STROSSMAN.

A hundred pounds to the man who disarms him.

FERSEN.

Death, not gold, you curs! take death for your reward.

Hans and the two men draw and make a dash at Fersen, but fall back awed.)

STROSSMAN (calls).

More men, I say ; disarm him at a rush !

(Two servants enter door L.)

FERSEN.

More cowards !   Then the more to die.

(They again attack Fersen ; the two men L. rush in and seize him from the back, and hold him in their arms.)

STROSSMAN (with exultation).

Ah, my fair lady, you will not escape my toils.   Victory at last !

(A loud knock at hall door—consternation and surprise.)

FERSEN.

No, scoundrel ; she is saved—saved !

STROSSMAN.

What does this mean ?

FERSEN.

Your guests are arriving ; go, and greet them.

STROSSMAN.

Curses on your infernal meddling !

FERSEN.

My counter-plot, which has destroyed your accursed scheme.

(Voice outside, "Sir Joshua Reynolds !" The men release Fersen, who turns to Angelica. Strossman with anger goes up stage.)
(To Angelica.)

You are saved, dear lady ! Bear yourself bravely—make a great effort ; no one will ever know of this shameful insult—no one *must* ever know. Your honour is without reproach.   You have arrived a little before the other guests, that's the explanation. Bravely ; sit on the sofa ; you will soon recover your self-possession. All is well now ; you are safe. I am only the valet Fersen once more. I shall watch over your safety, but, be assured, you shall not be compromised by my presence.

(He retires from her, and goes out R.; she sinks on settee.)

(Hans enters contre door, announces, "Sir Joshua Reynolds!" who appears in doorway C. Strossman advances to receive him; they bow with ceremony.)

SIR JOSHUA.

A thousand thanks, my dear Count, for your kind attention in sending notes to the theatre to remind us of this charming engagement. Very unnecessary—an invitation to Count Strossman's house could never be forgotten by the honoured recipient.

(Loud knock at hall door, voice outside announces, "Mr. Bartolozzi!")

We are all rather late. Much excitement at the theatre. I can assure you that "She Stoops to Conquer" is a great success, a true wholesome English comedy. If I can claim to be a judge, it's a play that will run twenty-five nights, at the very least, and even longer, I shouldn't wonder—ay, and be played again a dozen times next season.

(Hans enters and announces "Mr. Bartolozzi!" Bartolozzi enters, Strossman receives him; they bow with ceremony.)

BARTOLOZZI.

Well, Count, Dr. Goldsmith has had a great triumph. I'm in love with Miss Hardcastle, a true English girl— fresh, genuine nature—the sweetest girl I ever met. And then the fun of the plot! As for Dr. Johnson, why, his big laugh was heard all over the house—he actually thundered with laughter.

(Hans enters C., and announces "Lady Margaret Forbes! Miss Reynolds!" They enter; Strossman receives them with great ceremony.)

MISS REYNOLDS.

Well, Count, the great Doctor was right, after all.

STROSSMAN.

Madam, I humbly bow; your very unlearned servant
was wrong.

(Aside.)

Twice in one day that accursed fellow has defeated my
purpose, but the third time I shall be quits with him; and
that prudish minx shall be conquered, let the cost be what
it may.

(Miss Reynolds comes down stage to Angelica.)

MISS REYNOLDS.

Ah, Angelica, you ought to have been at the play with
us. Joshua has been as solemn as an owl, thinking and
moping all the evening. If you muddle it again, I'll
never forgive you. It's now or never for the nimble
"Yes."

(She turns up stage to Bartolozzi in conversation, and presently they
retire to the drawing-room; Lady Margaret converses with Strossman, Reynolds comes down stage and approaches Angelica.)

SIR JOSHUA.

Ah, Miss Angel, so you arrived before us?

ANGELICA (with effort).

Yes, Sir Joshua, a short time. The play must have
been very late.

(Aside.)

Oh, if he only knew the agony I have endured !

SIR JOSHUA.

A most amusing comedy. I wish you could have been
present; but you were right, art before all else.

(A pause.)

LADY MARGARET (to Strossman).

Look at them, I say; she attracts him like a magnet.
How will you avert this hateful marriage? It's too pro-
voking! You talk as women talk, and do nothing.

STROSSMAN (to Lady Margaret).

Nothing, you say! Ay, but I shall. The second string
—she loves my valet Fersen. A few minutes' patience,
you will see.

(To Hans.)

In the drawing-room, Hans. This way, my lady.

(Leads Lady Margaret into the drawing-room. Loud knock at hall
     door. Voice outside, " Mr. Topham Beauclerk, Mrs. Montague, Mr.
     Boswell !")

SIR JOSHUA (to Angelica).

Pardon me, but I'm sure you are suffering, your countenance is so troubled. You look as if you had passed
through some great ordeal, some terrible conflict. Confide
in me ; let me help you.

ANGELICA.

Nothing, nothing, I assure you. Well, it's very absurd,
but that little sketch for the ball invitations—it cost me
some trouble ; perhaps I was not quite in the mood for
artistic work, however insignificant.

(Hans conducts two gentlemen and a lady past the centre entrance—
     voice of Hans in drawing-room announcing " Mr. Topham Beauclerk,
     Mrs. Montague, Mr. Boswell !")

SIR JOSHUA.

No, no, my dear lady ; the sketch doesn't account for it.
Be frank with me ; perhaps my manner to you when we
parted this afternoon—the ridiculous fracas with that
impertinent valet—my manner might have been some-
what constrained, or even cold. I have thought much
this evening at the theatre—thoughts too deep for words.
I have scarcely even laughed at dear Goldie's clever fun.

ANGELICA.

Indeed, Sir Joshua, it is not in the slightest degree your
fault ; your manner is always most kind, most helpful to

my poor strivings in art. You are a sure friend, in whose honest opinion I can trust—a learned adviser in all my difficulties.

SIR JOSHUA.

Ay, ay, but let me be something more than that. Listen to me, Miss Angel—thoughts find words now. Let it be from friendship to love, and then from love to marriage— my wife !

ANGELICA (with exultation).

Your wife ! your wife !

SIR JOSHUA.

Yes; my *dear, honoured* wife !

ANGELICA (in changed tones).

A great honour—a great honour !

SIR JOSHUA.

Love, not honour ! A wife ! all is merged in that sacred name.

ANGELICA.

Yes, honour—always honour : the wife of Sir Joshua Reynolds !

(Starts up ; aside.)

Oh, strange short hour of a life—from lowest depths of shame to highest honour and reverence.

SIR JOSHUA.

Dearest lady, Angel mine, grant me a gracious answer.

ANGELICA.

It is all so sudden—do not press me ; I cannot answer now. I have lived hitherto for art alone. I cannot be so quickly faithless to my old allegiance. I deeply appreciate the honour you have done me. I am very unworthy. Nay, let me call you friend—always a friend—a valued friend !

SIR JOSHUA (in constrained tones).

Be it so, Miss Angel ; a friend, then—always a friend. Perhaps one day, at least, a friend not without hope.

(With a stately bow, Sir Joshua goes into drawing-room.)

ANGELICA.

Rejected! and my father's anxious purpose of a wise and eligible marriage destroyed by my own act. If he had made his offer this afternoon, I should have been his —saved from this past agony of shame ; but he makes his offer at a moment when love, mad, wild love, has entered my heart with resistless power. Oh, hero of noblest dreams of chivalry—true nobleman by virtue of noblest reverence for women—brave, unselfish, self-denying— come, if you will, and claim my heart. Alas! the valet Fersen, too proud to bend, too modest to claim a reward which he has won. He will never stoop to ask for a recompense. Why, then, it is for me to bend before a noble nature, for me to fling away the false trammels of society, to claim his heart of chivalry and devotion for my own.

(Fersen enters R., and comes down to Angelica.)

FERSEN.

Honoured lady, I have secured a coach for you. You will be guarded by two devoted comrades; they will conduct you safely home. To linger here must be an intolerable agony. You have been seen by all the company; you can safely withdraw on the plea of indisposition. I pray you to let this evening be blotted from your mind. You must forget all the persons who have been involved in this past wickedness—ay, whether for good or evil, it is well and right that you should forget it all—too infamous a recollection for an honourable woman's memory !

ANGELICA.

One—will never be forgotten.

4

FERSEN.

Even that one, I say, who bitterly repents his mad presumption this morning; the valet Fersen, how should he have dared?

ANGELICA.

Let him dare.

FERSEN.

What! may he hope?

ANGELICA.

Yes—hope.

FERSEN.

Hope to win a name and fame? But these will come too late—you will have married, and fame will be a bitter mockery.

ANGELICA.

I will never marry—my solemn pledge—so long as I may hope to become your wife, be that time long or short.

FERSEN.

Angelica, my angel! Too much joy, too much joy for heart and brain! it will kill me! But your father?—he will compel you to marry.

ANGELICA.

My pledge to you; I am strong enough to resist my father's importunities. I will reject every suitor till my great hope be at an end, and then—what matter?—my father may have his will—I will marry at his command— but not my heart—not my heart.

FERSEN.

Oh, glorious hope! Heaven's fullest blessing to redress the hardships of my life—nay, Heaven's mercy! It was for this I lost title and honour; it was for this I was denied name and heritage. Oh, glorious recompense!—a loss by which I have gained the noblest woman in the world!

Dear plighted wife! then some time I may press you to my heart, some time kiss those lips with the betrothal kiss—Heaven's blessing on a sacred pledge.

> (Servant enters R., crosses stage to L., and, standing in door-way, announces, "Supper is served." Confused murmurs in drawing-room L., and cries of "Fersen! Fersen!")

What's that? What do they want with me in this moment of joy?

> (Voice of Strossman followed by other voices. "Long live the Count de Horne! Long live the Count de Horne!")

Count de Horne! Heaven, is it possible? Not now—not now; happiness gained for a moment and lost for ever.

> (Strossman enters L. with Lady Margaret on his arm, followed by Sir Joshua conducting a lady, Bartolozzi, Miss Reynolds and other guests. Strossman on seeing Fersen stops in centre of stage and addresses him.)

STROSSMAN.

Ah, Fersen, I have sent to request your presence. I have a great announcement to make: no longer Fersen my valet. Ladies and gentlemen, I have the honour to present to you Count de Horne—in the kingdom of Sweden, among our nobles, the third in rank!

> (To Fersen.)

I have just received an important despatch—the Royal Courts have recognised the nobility of your mother's descent: you are restored to the family titles and honours. I am ordered by the despatch to treat you with the honour due to your rank—money, ample credit, henceforth at your command. I am your humble servant, at your bidding.

> (Bows)

Long live the Count de Horne!

> (Guests echo the cry. Strossman and Lady Margaret pass into the supper-room —the other guests gather round Fersen with congratula-tions; they gradually retire into supper-room R., and Fersen is left alone with Angelica.)

ANGELICA.

Count de Horne, a thousand congratulations! You are worthy of your great title—noble by birthright, as you have ever been by nature.

FERSEN.

Alas! you know not what you say. Despair! The glorious hope is lost for ever! Oh, dearest lady!—oh, plighted wife! snatched from my arms as surely as if Death had flung his relentless dart—I can never marry you!

ANGELICA.

As fatal as that? In mercy, is there no hope?

FERSEN.

Those cruel laws of arrogance and pride divide us for ever.

ANGELICA.

Defy them! Love's defiance! What care we for laws?

FERSEN.

Impossible!—alas, impossible!

ANGELICA.

Impossible? Not that fatal word! There must be some remedy.

FERSEN.

No remedy but shame. You cannot be my wife! I dare not whisper that vile word " mistress."

(Angelica starts back.)

Have no fear; honour shall divide us, not shame. And yet—oh, maddening thought to lose you now—to lose you for ever! Your presence is so dear and sweet to me; Angelica, we cannot part. Nay, dearest; some sure refuge, unknown to the world—alone—together—always true! What am I saying? An insult! I read it in your face. Bid me go—no; tell me to stay. Nay, as between us, a holy love, no shame—always honourable, always noble in my eyes—the idol of my heart!

ANGELICA.

The idol of your heart, but dragged down to shame by your own hands—nothing left to worship—a woman to despise.

FERSEN.

What have I said ? Is the curse of this den of infamy laid upon me, tainting with dishonour every word of my lips ? Bid me go, I say—speak, and I will obey. Nay, do not speak—not that fatal word, which divides us for ever. Oh, sweetest love, do we live for the world—this false, cruel world? We live for one another. The world of our love is large enough for life—a kingdom of happiness without bounds ! What's the world to us ?

ANGELICA.

Nothing.

FERSEN (with passion).

Then mine for ever—queen of my world !

ANGELICA (shrinking back).

I said the world was nothing—scorn, dishonour, bitter words, a heavy burden of shame. I could bear it all before the world—my love for you would give me strength; but in your sight, alone with you, I could never bear that burden, I'm too weak for that—fallen in the eyes of the man I love ! Loved, I know it, but pitied. The pity of your eyes would kill me ! the crimson of shame would dye my face, every kiss would burn my lips ! Our world a kingdom of disgrace, not happiness ! Go, if so it must be; let honour divide us, not shame. Go, I beg and pray —go, because I love you.

FERSEN.

Forgive me for the words I have uttered. No safety for honour but in flight.

(Murmurs in supper-room, "Miss Kauffmann.")

They come to seek you. You will be safe among so many friends. Farewell—farewell for ever !

(Exit 1st entrance L. Angelica starts up dazed, and gazes after him.)

ANGELICA.

It cannot be! Some fearful dream! Lover—husband—— No; snatched from my arms—like death! nay, worse than death—living, yet dead to me!

(Sinks down on settee ; Sir Joshua appears at entrance R.)

SIR JOSHUA.

Miss Kauffmann! Everyone is asking for Miss Kauffmann!

(He comes down stage.)

CURTAIN.

ACT III.

SIR JOSHUA'S BRIDE.

(Lapse of a month between Acts II. and III.)

SCENE.

Same as Act I. Lady Margaret Forbes discovered painting at easel. Strossman enters immediately after rise of curtain; he bows to Lady Margaret.

LADY MARGARET.

Well, Count, these cobweb schemes of yours? Time marches apace; in three days Angelica will become the wife of Sir Joshua.

STROSSMAN.

But you admit that she loves De Horne?

LADY MARGARET.

Youth before age and fame: I know it. She treats Sir Joshua, the man I adore with my whole heart and soul, as a second string to love's bow. Congratulations fall thick upon her, and proud smiles and blushes mantle her countenance — the bride of a great English artist; and then, as she averts her face from the crowd, tears gather in her eyes.

STROSSMAN.

So we hold the King of Hearts among our cards!

LADY MARGARET.

You harp for ever on the old string. Once more I say she cannot marry De Horne.

STROSSMAN.

If they cannot marry, what harm in their meeting?
Urge that point on Miss Kauffmann, in mercy to the
young Count. Let them meet in that full conviction—to
refuse would be unheard-of cruelty; no woman could
deal so hardly with a hapless lover. Let them meet, I
say, only once, and leave the rest to me. Sir Joshua shall
be yours to wed—if you can win him; Angelica will be
mine, at my feet by to-morrow's sun. Have faith; I
never lose my game when I play for love.

LADY MARGARET.

Tell me this plan of yours—a mystery?

STROSSMAN.

Nay, let me keep my secret. Well, a woman's heart—
call it a harpsichord: I have the magic touch—a cunning
of my own—the keys are responsive to my will. Ensure
me this interview, and give me free access to your house
—it's all the help I need. I will retire to the library when
I desire to be alone.

LADY MARGARET.

My house is at your command; but pray avoid Angelica,
your presence always seems to alarm her.

STROSSMAN.

A prejudice easily conquered; she'll cling to me before
long.
                                        (Enter servant.)

SERVANT.

Madame Blanche waits on your ladyship and Miss
Kauffmann by appointment.
                                        (Exit servant.)

LADY MARGARET.

I must leave you, Count; the dressmaker—the dresses
for this *hateful* wedding; you see, there is no time to be
lost.

STROSSMAN.

I said to-morrow ; no time shall be lost.

(They bow ; Lady Margaret goes out.)

Farewell, my lady ; the dressmaker has intervened most conveniently ; I want to be alone in this room for a few minutes. Angelica really loyes Fersen ; I knew it in the fiasco of that supper ! I shan't fail twice. But she cannot wed him as a noble ; true, quite true, that's the law of Sweden—and he *is* a noble, as this decree shows

(Draws parchment document from his pocket)

most conclusively, drawn in sound legal form, and pur-porting to be duly issued from the Royal Chancery, but as yet not authenticated by royal seal. And now to find the seal—old Kauffmann's work-table !

(Goes to table near C. window with engraver's appliances on it, and a taper burning.)

Ah, here we find it ; and the forged seal—here it is,

(Takes up seal)

and several test impressions—excellent as legal evidences of fraud. A good die-sinker, on my word ! Most oppor-tune that Mr. Bartolozzi was unable to execute the secret commission, and so transferred the work to his old friend. And now to seal the document. Ah, useful taper !

(Takes up wax, melts at candle, and seals document.)

So ! authenticated at last by the great seal of Sweden. Good workmanship, Mr. Kauffmann, but it's dangerous work to fabricate royal seals—the penalty is death, I fancy. Angelica, my goddess, have no fear ; I will save your father's life when he lies fast and close in Newgate Gaol. I win this *coup*, Angelica, doubly sure—father and daughter in my grasp.

(Listens.)

Ah, the good old Kauffmann returns to his labours. I'll to my books in the library.

(Exit into library. Enter Kauffmann, speaking back.)

KAUFFMANN.

One peep, my child, at the bridal dress when it is fitted on. Your old father is so happy, so happy!

(Turns to table.)

I must to my work; Signor Bartolozzi will be here directly; I promised that the seal should be ready to-day. But my child's wedding-dress—Sir Joshua's bride; every fold must be worthy of his brush—sweeps of drapery in graceful lines; and underneath no lay figure, dull and cold, but flesh and blood, a living picture for an artist's arms.

(Bartolozzi enters.)

Ah, the dear Bartolozzi; you've come in the nick of time for a rare sight.

BARTOLOZZI.

Is the seal finished, old friend? Business first.

KAUFFMANN.

Almost.

(Takes up seal) ˙

A little more polish, and I'm off to the ivory-turner.

BARTOLOZZI.

It must be delivered to-day.

KAUFFMANN.

You're sure you hold a safe commission for its execution? It looks like some royal seal—a coat-of-arms and a crown—it would be forgery, would it not?

BARTOLOZZI.

You can trust me. I hold the order for its execution from the Ambassador of the State to which it belongs, signed by his own hand. But this rare sight——

KAUFFMANN.

Angelica in her wedding-dress. It's my design—a rich harmony of gold and bronze, yet sober. They are to go to church without fuss and parade, and they are to go off from the church down to Richmond Hill for the honeymoon. Sir Joshua hates the thought of a gaping crowd.

BARTOLOZZI.

Well, old friend, it's a right good match for our Angelica.

KAUFFMANN.

Ay, ay, but for that cursed law of Sweden she might have been a great Countess. Poor young man! I know how deeply he loves her—begs and prays me to let him see her for one last interview; but Angelica refuses to see him.

BARTOLOZZI.

Angelica is right—steadfast in her love and loyalty to Sir Joshua.

KAUFFMANN.

But a Countess—a Countess! She's the idol of my life!

(Angelica enters.)

Nothing too good or too noble for her; she's worthy of the highest honour!

BARTOLOZZI.

The hand of a great artist!

ANGELICA (coming down).

A far greater honour than Angelica deserves.

KAUFFMANN.

Angelica, my angel. Now, Bartolozzi, gaze and praise. Grandly, my child—stately pose; here, these folds—one moment.

(Arranges her dress.)

My design, but these dressmakers are not artists. Still, the intention is not wholly lost, and the colour is all my own.

BARTOLOZZI.

A triumph, Kauffmann, worthy of Sir Joshua's magic
brush !

KAUFFMANN.

Worthy of a coronet, I say.

ANGELICA.

What are coronets to me ? We artists rise, if we can,
and win our crowns of fame—patents given by our own
hands. I am but a poor handmaid in art; but he, the
man I love, stoops from his vantage-ground, and raises
me to share his name and fame. Can kings give higher
honour ? A husband to esteem and love, a master to
instruct, and the world will say of Angelica's work, " the
sweetness was her own, but the grace and strength she
gained were her husband's gifts, though weakly rendered
by a woman's hand." That's honour enough for me !

BARTOLOZZI.

Hold to that, Angelica mine, yet bear your honours with
a smile; don't let this weight of honour subdue your
lighter nature ; he'll love you for the smiles, this master
of woman's sweetest moods—the light and shade of a
woman's face, if you will, not always shadow.

ANGELICA.

Dear Bartolozzi, I am subdued ; I can't help it ; love
has come to my heart in sober garb, and yet with great
joy.
(Tears come into her eyes.)
Well, tears of joy; and just now—this dress, perhaps—
marriage seems so solemn as the day approaches. You've
had your peep, dear father ; I'll change the dress, and be
Angelica once more—your own daughter, who owes everything to your love and devotion !

(Kisses Kauffmann.)

KAUFFMANN.

Angel mine, always my sweet Angel !
(Wipes his eyes.)
I'm an old fool ! None of your laughing, Bartolozzi !

BARTOLOZZI.

I love to see your happiness, old friend. She's my god-daughter ; I'm as big a fool as her real father !
(Enter Miss Reynolds.)

MISS REYNOLDS.

I can't endure my Lady Margaret any longer. The dressmaker's having a warm time of it, I warrant you.
(To Kauffmann.)
I like your design vastly well, Mr. Kauffmann—rich, and flowing, and artistic. I'm sure Joshua will be delighted.

BARTOLOZZI (to Kauffmann).

Come, you've had praise enough ; let's to the ivory man and finish this seal business. We've dealt with the dress as costume and colour ; let's leave the ladies to deal with the snippings and pinnings ! Ladies, your most obedient.
(Bartolozzi and Kauffmann go out.)

MISS REYNOLDS.

Yes, a very handsome dress ; but to my taste it's a little too serious for a wedding-dress.

ANGELICA.

But, recollect, it's a travelling-dress, and Sir Joshua——

MISS REYNOLDS (with emphasis).

Joshua !

ANGELICA.

Joshua !

MISS REYNOLDS.

Say " dear Joshua "—let me hear you distinctly !

ANGELICA.

" Dear Joshua !"

MISS REYNOLDS.

Well, there, I never saw such a pair of lovers—Miss Angelica Kauffmann and Sir Joshua Reynolds. Loves and doves, and bliss and kiss, not a bit of it—all so stiff, and courtly, and stately. Why, you demure darling! love isn't a minuet of bows and scrapings.

ANGELICA.

But your brother—consider his position in art.

MISS REYNOLDS.

Well, it isn't my idea of love, but perhaps you're right; the lips he loves to paint have always scared him back to the covert of his painting-room. As to lovers' talk of sweet nothings, not one word; but placid converse as to composition and outline, faint breathings of chiaroscuro, murmurs of scumblings and glazings, lispings of varnish —he was doomed to die a bachelor, if he hadn't met a woman whose only passion was her love of art.

ANGELICA.

Say, at least, that her passion was her love and reverence for her husband's greatness!

MISS REYNOLDS.

Pooh! pooh! I do love to tease you both. My Joshua —he's very great, of course; but to me he's the sweetest, and the kindest, and the most generous man that ever lived. I know you feel that too.

ANGELICA.

I know it—I know it; would that I were really worthy of his love!

(Cries.)

MISS REYNOLDS.

You are, dearest. Come, come, no tears!
(Sir Joshua enters.)
Why, by all that's wonderful, here's Joshua! I've made

your bride-elect cry, wicked Fanny as I am. Give her a kiss, Joshua, and set it right.

SIR JOSHUA.

Dearest!

(Kisses Angelica's hand.)

MISS REYNOLDS.

Lips, Joshua, lips.

SIR JOSHUA (in courtly tone).

Miss Kauffmann.

MISS REYNOLDS.

" Angelica," Joshua! When shall I ever teach you to say " Angelica "?

SIR JOSHUA.

Angelica, my darling, as dear, wicked Fanny insists——

(Kisses Angelica in stately way.)

MISS REYNOLDS.

Pooh, Joshua! that's the way to kiss a sister, not a bride. Let me.

(Kisses Angelica.)

Strong in the mouth, love on the lips!

SIR JOSHUA.

But respect in the heart as well as love, Fanny; and Angelica——

ANGELICA.

Is assured of this love. What but love could have caused an artist to desert his painting-room at this hour of the day, to be false to his sweet mistress, Art—noble as she is sweet—to come courting a poor foolish woman, a thing of whims and worries—ripples on the surface of his placid life!

MISS REYNOLDS.

Well, it isn't my sort of love, but I'm glad you like it. Give me Romeo and Mr. Garrick, swearing and tearing; Juliet and Mrs. Cibber, sighing and crying.

SIR JOSHUA.

Fanny, consider, a Romeo rather hard of hearing, and a Juliet who has won her laurels, who has gained the highest honour in her profession.

ANGELICA.

What do you mean?

SIR JOSHUA.

Miss Angelica Kauffmann, Royal Academician.

ANGELICA.

Impossible!

SIR JOSHUA.

Your diploma signed this morning.

(Gives paper to Angelica.)

ANGELICA.

But your gift—awarded to me for your sake; my honour, but gained by your merit!

(Kisses Sir Joshua with fervour.)

SIR JOSHUA.

There, Fanny, Juliet has kissed Romeo—is this love?

ANGELICA.

Love, and admiration, and gratitude.

MISS REYNOLDS (with a bow to Angelica).

I congratulate Miss Angelica Kauffmann, R.A.—Lady Reynolds elect.

ANGELICA.

The higher honour!

(Gives her hand to Sir Joshua.)

MISS REYNOLDS.

Well, I must go back to my Lady Margaret and protect the dressmaker, or it will be murder.

ANGELICA.

And I also.

MISS REYNOLDS.

You have your excuse, Angelica, a lover—a pair of lovers, a pair of paint-brushes in love! How Signor Cupid must laugh at your courtship—maulsticks instead of arrows!

(Exit Miss Reynolds.)

ANGELICA.

Dear Fanny, she loves her joke. But why not love in sober reason instead of unreason? Not wild random love without valid cause—the mad love which ends in despair, which flings wisdom and consequences to the wind!

SIR JOSHUA.

Angel mine, no matter how it came about. You came to me; I was alone, and like to have been alone to the end of my life; you came to me with the love of my love —art—with the sympathy which is born of common knowledge, of common aspirations. The ignorance of other women, gazing idly at the canvas, would have been a perpetual worry; and empty chatter often pains my ears; but you would stand at my side, and you would feel, as I feel, every touch of the brush, its meaning and its purpose, as clear to you as to me—a silent converse, sweeter than spoken words.

ANGELICA.

Honoured beyond all women!

SIR JOSHUA.

Loved! Your painting-room will be next to mine.

ANGELICA.

Master and pupil.

SIR JOSHUA.

Nay, fellow-students, Angelica. In the great school of art we are always students. And you will be my sweet model—always Angelica, like Andrea del Sarto's wife.

ANGELICA.

But she was faithless !

SIR JOSHUA.

But he loved her—he had no choice, love's tyranny was too strong. Those dreams of mine that wait realization—the unpainted pictures of the brain—I have found my perfect model at last. But this new dress ?

ANGELICA.

I never meant you to see it till I stood at the altar—my wedding-dress.

SIR JOSHUA.

I like it—this rich gold and brown.

ANGELICA.

My father's design.

SIR JOSHUA.

Very pleasant, and full of rich harmonies—flowing drapery. Sit, darling.

(She sits in sitter's chair.)

I have it, an old fancy of mine which has been lurking in my brain many a year—the Muse of Art. Let me place you in the pose I have imagined—so, sweet one !

(He arranges her attitude in accordance with that of Mrs. Siddons as the Tragic Muse.)

Asphalt and crimson-lake for richness and depth, then glazings of gamboge. Don't move awhile, dearest. What a courtship for a painter—you and I together ! Love's commission ! The smiles I love to paint, my own ; given to me—your heart's gift ; and the eyes, the language of the soul poured out for me. What inspiration for an artist ! It will be my great work, Angelica ; they shall gaze on it in the after days, when this hand is dust ; his masterpiece, they'll say, for Love was the master who inspired the work. What ! tears, darling, tears ?

Yes, tears—tears.

(She sinks from the chair and kneels at his feet.)

Oh, Heaven! make me worthy of this great love and honour, guard me from all temptation. I have been a flirt—inconstant. Nay, let me speak the whole truth to you; and now I am face to face with nobleness and steadfastness, and I tremble for my poor weak nature, a vain, frivolous woman—I cannot be sure of myself!

SIR JOSHUA *(raises her tenderly)*.

I can—love makes us strong and true. I know you love me. I know you will never be false to your heart, be the sacrifice what it may.

(Miss Reynolds enters.)

ANGELICA.

Never—never!

(Aside.)

Heaven help me!

MISS REYNOLDS.

It's time to be off, Joshua. I've saved the milliner's life. I'm not sure it was worth saving! Bless me! love makes you forget your appointments—Dr. Johnson will be waiting for his sitting. Hey-dey! why, you've made your bride cry yourself—the "Mourning Bride." It's very fine, but give me comedies—"Love for Love"—bright and light—the love that laughs.

SIR JOSHUA.

Steadfast and true, Fanny—husband and wife—the love that endures. Farewell, Angel; Dr. Johnson's time is too valuable to be lost, even for a lover's happiness. Don't forget the dinner-hour in Leicester Square—you and your father, Fanny and self, Dr. Johnson and Dr. Goldsmith. Dear Goldie, he'll make us laugh—comedy for this evening, that's sure!

MISS REYNOLDS.

Farewell, bride elect! Fanny is longing to resign the power of the keys into your hands!

ANGELICA.

Would they were worthier hands!

SIR JOSHUA.

The worthiest a man could desire, the fairest a painter could paint! Henceforth these hands will be my models. Farewell, Angel mine—but only till this evening.

(Miss Reynolds goes to door. Sir Joshua clasps Angelica in his arms and kisses her forehead.)

MISS REYNOLDS.

Kiss her again—lips, Joshua, always lips! Real lips don't smudge like paint!

(Sir Joshua kisses Angelica's lips.)

That's a kiss at last, a warrantable kiss! Now, come along quick, or Dr. Johnson will begin to growl like a bear.

(Miss Reynolds and Sir Joshua go out. Angelica throws herself into a chair at the table and clasps her hands over her face. A pause.)

ANGELICA.

I do love him—I do love him! How can I help loving him—so kind, so sweet, so gentle, so great? I know his greatness. I have seen great men's works, dead and gone —I have weighed their greatness, and he is as great as they are great; and yet he's so humble—a student still. Mine, this genius; mine, his honour and renown; mine, his grand humility! Lady Reynolds—his wife! What a crown of honour for a woman to wear! What's it made of, this heart of mine, dull lead, cold marble? No response. Does my soul rush to the lips when his lips kiss mine? No spark of fervour, no flame of love! Burnt out, the past? No; still there. That image is still graven there, strive to hide it as I may, holding my heart with resistless

force. I cannot marry that man—it never can be—hopeless, impossible! Then why repine? Why vainly sorrow
through long sleepless hours of the night? Why, he
saved me from fatal sleep, and now I cannot sleep, and
wakefulness of sorrow repays my debt to him. But for
his image, I could love Sir Joshua with my whole heart.
Perhaps time—— Time's a slow physician—I must bear
the torture till time does its work of mercy.

(Kauffmann enters, followed by Lady Margaret. Angelica starts
to her feet.)

Oh, father mine, dearest father, such honour! Have
you heard?

KAUFFMANN.

No, Angelica, my own!

ANGELICA.

Your daughter a Royal Academician! Just think of it
—a woman, a Royal Academician!

KAUFFMANN.

A woman! but art knows no sex!

(Embraces her.)

My darling child—your old father—he reaps his reward:
his child's honour—the crown of his old age.

LADY MARGARET (interposing).

A thousand congratulations, dear Angelica.

ANGELICA (with forced exultation).

Thanks. Lady Margaret, a thousand thanks; no congratulations can be too great for my great fortune. What
honour greater than the love of the great man who has
chosen me to be his wife? The thought half turns my
head with joy and exultation. Dearest father, words
can't tell the joy and pride I feel: he is so good, so noble!

LADY MARGARET.

Angelica, dearest, forgive me, I have a request to make. You are so happy now, so full of assured happiness, that perhaps you might spare some little sympathy for one who suffers deep sorrow for your sake.

ANGELICA.

What do you mean?

LADY MARGARET.

Count de Horne!
(Angelica starts and shudders.)
He prays one last interview, one last farewell. He leaves England immediately—this very day, perhaps.

ANGELICA.

I have written to him the kindest letter I could write; but I cannot see him. Once for all, I will not see him.

LADY MARGARET.

But, in reason, tell me why?

ANGELICA.

An interview can only be painful to him.

LADY MARGARET.

But not painful to you. Your heart is full of joyful love for your affianced husband; spare him a little sympathy and pity; he sorely needs it, poor young man!

ANGELICA.

Is he so—so very——

LADY MARGARET.

Cast down in the depths of despair. He only seeks to bid you one eternal farewell; at least, you might grant him that small consolation.

ANGELICA.

But Sir Joshua--he would not——

LADY MARGARET.

Sir Joshua is too generous to object to an act of kindness and mercy. I repeat, Count de Horne cannot marry you; if he were in that position, depend on it, I should not be his advocate, in common justice to Sir Joshua Reynolds and yourself.

ANGELICA.

I will not see him. Let this matter cease.

KAUFFMANN.

My child, he has begged and prayed me to ask you to grant him this one last interview; his prayers are so persistent, I do think you might grant him this small mercy.

ANGELICA.

Father, I will not listen to another word on the subject. Go to him—I insist!—and tell him my determination. His persistence is unmanly and cruel! Go, I say, find him, and end this painful affair. Go, if you love me— go!

(Kauffmann goes out.)

LADY MARGARET.

Why, dear Angelica, one would think you doubted your own heart!

ANGELICA.

Doubt my own heart? That's Sir Joshua's! This young man, what is he to me?

LADY MARGARET.

If nothing, then why not see him?

ANGELICA.

I will not! Once for all.

LADY MARGARET.

Brave words! If the truth were told, I believe you dare not!

ANGELICA.

Dare?

LADY MARGARET.

Dare not, I repeat—because, in your inmost heart, I believe you love him.

ANGELICA.

Take care, Lady Margaret, words of this nature will destroy our friendship. See him? of course I can see him. But why such useless pain to him? He's nothing to me, I repeat—utterly indifferent. If you dare me in this way, I will see him.

(Enter servant.)

SERVANT.

The Count de Horne waits on your ladyship.

LADY MARGARET.

Announce the Count, when I ring.

(Exit servant.)

ANGELICA.

This is some design, some cruel plot.

LADY MARGARET.

Your conduct is absurd. You say he is nothing to you —let me ring the bell—the interview will be over in a few minutes; he will be consoled, and you will be spared all further importunity.

(Goes towards bell. Angelica strives to hold her back.)

ANGELICA.

No—no! spare me! spare me! I can't see him! I will not see him!

LADY MARGARET.

Don't hold my hands in this rough way!

(Breaks from Angelica and rings bell.)

ANGELICA.

I won't see him, I say! I'll lock myself into my own room till he leaves the house !

(Goes towards door.)

LADY MARGARET.

You'll meet him in the hall.

ANGELICA.

Through the library, then !

(She goes to library door, enters, utters a cry, and flies back.)

Oh, horror ! Count Strossman !

(Servant enters and announces " The Count de Horne." Fersen enters, servant retires.)

FERSEN.

Miss Kauffmann—Angelica !

(He advances towards her, she shrinks back.)

ANGELICA (in broken, hurried voice, standing at bay.)

Why do you come in defiance of my refusals? I say it is unmanly to persecute me in this determined way. Well, you have come, and to what end? You are Count de Horne, I am Angelica Kauffmann, the affianced wife of Sir Joshua Reynolds; that fact ends everything.

FERSEN.

I have only desired one last interview before leaving this country for ever. My route is prepared for Harwich. I only wait for the legal document from the Swedish Embassy confirming my restitution in blood; I leave London immediately on its receipt. Oh, Angelica, you are happy in your coming marriage, be generous, and spare a little pity for one who is doomed henceforth to bear an eternal sorrow in his heart.

ANGELICA.

You go to wealth and honour, a great nobleman in your own land—what more for a man's ambition ?

FERSEN.

I leave the treasure of my life behind. I cannot speak
as I would speak—as I must speak. Lady Margaret,
grant us a few minutes alone.

ANGELICA.

Lady Margaret, do not leave this room, I beg and
pray.

LADY MARGARET.

Only a few minutes. What harm in a few minutes'
conversation ?

ANGELICA.

In justice to me—in justice to Sir Joshua.

LADY MARGARET.

I shall be in the library, close at hand.
(Goes to the library door.)

ANGELICA.

You shall stay, or I will go.
(Follows Lady Margaret towards library, then starts back, aside.)
Count Strossman ! Is there no refuge left ?

FERSEN (with fervour).

Ah, Angelica, why afraid of me ? Was I not true to
you in that dark hour of your life ? Did I not save you
from shame and disgrace ? I make no boast, but through
my devotion, you will go to the altar and wed your husband as an honourable bride. Is this not true ?

ANGELICA.

It is—it is.
(Aside.)
Heaven help me !

FERSEN.

And now—now that I cannot marry you, forbidden by
those accursed laws, with a burning passion in my bosom,

with endless wealth at my command, I do not seek you with false deluding words, and urge you to be my mistress if you cannot be my wife—disgrace to the woman I reverence and adore. Then why fear me?—why shun me? Why not let me bear away one gracious remembrance of this final interview? Be merciful! You go your way to happiness, a happy marriage with the man you love, I go my way to solitude and sorrow.

ANGELICA.

Leave me—leave me. I cannot—I must not—talk with you.

(She sits at table, clasping her hands over her face.)

FERSEN.

What! no better words than coldness and scorn—no poor words of simple gratitude, of common sympathy? Is this your nature? is this your heart? Hard to be borne, and bitter for the soul, but I thank you, madam, for this interview; it has taught me that the woman I loved was an ideal of my own creation; that the woman I thought I loved possessed a heart of stone. You can summon Lady Margaret, our interview is at an end. Farewell, madam, for ever!

(He moves towards door; Angelica, who has striven to restrain her feelings, bursts into violent sobs.)

ANGELICA (bitterly).

Tears from a heart of stone!

FERSEN (returning to her).

Angelica, it is not true; you are playing some false part—disguising your heart. Your tears speak the truth —you love me—love me!

ANGELICA (starting up).

I love you—I *do* love you. I never knew how much I loved you till this hour. I felt I must hide from your presence, that then I might wrench away the feeling; but I never knew its strength till now!

FERSEN.

Angelica!

ANGELICA.

No lie shall stand between us in this last interview. I do love you, my hero, my protector; bear away that thought. And bear away this thought also, that you have honoured and revered the woman you love. Go forth into the world; remember your exalted position; do great works and noble deeds!

FERSEN.

I might—I think I might—but all energy in me is paralyzed; fame is.not love!

ANGELICA.

But duty and honour remain, work for them—men have stern work to do. Make me proud in the thought that I have loved you. Be brave and strong; be true to your own noble nature. Leave me with these words buried among our hearts' treasures—this last interview of honour. Farewell!

(Holds out her hand for him to kiss, he clasps it.)

FERSEN.

Grant my last prayer—your lips!—the death of our love, the last cold kiss of death.
        (She lets him kiss her.)
My lost love! my lost love! Farewell! I will give you no more useless pain. I bless you for the consolation of this parting—" Proud in the thought that I have loved you." Farewell, Angelica!

(He kneels at her feet, kissing her hand; she lays her other hand on his head in solemn attitude; he rises, turns, and goes silently towards the door. Lady Margaret enters from library.)

LADY MARGARET.

Pardon my intrusion, but Count Strossman desires to see Count de Horne forthwith.

(Strossman enters.)

FERSEN (to Strossman).

I have forbidden you to enter this lady's presence.

STROSSMAN.

A hundred apologies, but here is the important document. I learnt that you were paying your respects to Lady Margaret. It has just been received at the Embassy. This decree declares you ennobled in blood, a high count of the kingdom of Sweden.

(Gives document to Fersen.)

FERSEN.

A noble, but the final end of all hope! Would that I were Fersen still! Would that it were false—some shameful forgery!

STROSSMAN.

It bears its own authenticity, the great seal of Sweden.

FERSEN (looks at seal).

The great seal of Sweden truly enough. Count de Horne, by solemn decree. Oh, mother, dear mother, restored to all the honours of your rank! Your son rejoices for your sake; he sorrows for his own.

(Suddenly to Strossman.)

Why do you linger, sir, still in this lady's presence? Begone, at once!

STROSSMAN (bowing).

I obey, Mr. de Horne.

FERSEN.

Mr. de Horne! What do you mean? I am by rank the third greatest nobleman in Sweden—Count de Horne, under this seal.

STROSSMAN.

Pardon me, sir, read carefully the terms of the decree. From to-morrow—the date of the decree is to-morrow, the 25th June, 1769—from to-morrow, you are ennobled in blood, but to-day you are merely a commoner, without any of the rights and privileges of nobility. Saving the presence of these ladies, I, as a noble of the third class, cover my head in your presence.

(Puts on his hat.)

Mr. de Horne to-day, to-morrow Count de Horne in all his dignity and honour.

(He bows to the ladies, and goes towards door; Fersen stops him.)

FERSEN.

You say I am only a commoner to-day?

STROSSMAN.

A simple commoner!

FERSEN (with intense agitation).

Then—then—tell me——

STROSSMAN.

I know what you would ask. I hurried to you, for there was no time to be lost. Small thanks have I received! You know our laws—the patent of nobility ennobles a commoner and his wife from the date of creation; but, from and after that date, a noble can only wed a bride of noble birth. To-day, you are free to wed as you will, and to-morrow you and your wedded wife become ennobled in blood—Count and Countess by the law of Sweden.

FERSEN.

Angelica!

(Angelica has listened intently during this dialogue; she stands transfixed with her hands in painful tension.)

STROSSMAN.

The canonical hour is not yet passed ; the priest is still
to be found in the Roman Catholic chapel close at hand,
in Farm Street. But time flies ; in half an hour marriage
will be impossible until to-morrow,

(Takes off his hat.)

and to-morrow will be too late for your marriage with a
commoner.

(Bows.)

Ladies, your most obedient !

(Aside on threshold.)

The battle is won ! Angelica will be mine.

(Exit.)

FERSEN (passionately).

Angelica, not death—life !—love ! All he says is true.
I know the law. You will rise with me—my honoured
wife ; but now, at once.

ANGELICA.

This is madness ! I am affianced to another. Impossible ! A crime !—perjury unmeasured !

FERSEN.

But you love me !

(Lady Margaret steals out of the room.)

ANGELICA.

But I'm engaged to another, I say. Plighted--pledged.
Leave me—in mercy, leave me !

FERSEN.

With love in your heart ? You swore you loved me !

ANGELICA.

I said so, but I said more than I meant. I was cajoled
into seeing you. I was prayed by others—by my father
even—to be kind in my manner, to give you some consolation ; but—well, I spoke words I really did not mean

—not in their fulness; things are changed now. Go!
Leave me, if you have any generosity, leave me, or I shall
hate you. Once for all, my hand belongs to another—it's
irrevocable—a plighted word—a bond of honour.

FERSEN.

That kiss!

ANGELICA.

Which ended all between us—a sacred kiss of death.
Go, I beg and pray.
(Calls.)
Lady Margaret, tell this man to leave this house; his
presence is an insult to me. Lady Margaret, I insist.

FERSEN.

Lady Margaret has left the room.

ANGELICA.

This is some plot, some shameful scheme.

FERSEN.

Cruel and unjust. Have I ever been untrue? Have I
ever sought you unworthily? Once more, remember that
dark hour! Cruel woman, is this my reward?

ANGELICA.

I cannot tell what I say! My brain is dazed. You see
my anguish—go, leave me. Why am I to be tortured
thus? Your love is cruelty and pain!

FERSEN.

I will go, never to see you again, on this condition.
Tell me, looking at me steadfastly in the face, that you do
not love me; that all your profession of love was a lie to
deceive me in my despair—to dismiss me with a falsehood
cherished in my heart. Speak those words, and I leave
you for ever.

ANGELICA (with supreme effort).

I say, " I do not love you ; all my profession of love was a lie."

FERSEN.

To deceive me.

ANGELICA.

" To deceive you."

FERSEN.

In my despair.

ANGELICA.

" In your despair."
(Suddenly in vehement tones.)

No—no ; I love you ! Perjured, false, unworthy, I love you ! honour or dishonour, life or death ! Heaven help me, I cannot help myself !

FERSEN.

Life and honour, my wife !
(He clasps her in his arms. Enter Lady Margaret.)
Lady Margaret, Angelica is mine. I have won the precious jewel of my coronet !

ANGELICA (to Lady Margaret).

False, perjured, unworthy, not mistress of myself, yet knowing right and wrong, but helpless to do right, compelled by some awful power. Tell him—tell Sir Joshua he must never look upon my face again. In mercy to him, have no mercy when you speak of me—despicable, frivolous, a jilt—well saved from such a wife : tell him at once, without delay—promise me !

FERSEN.

Come, Angelica, dearest wife, not this self-reproach. Love has conquered ; you have been true to your heart. The precious minutes fly—come !

6

ANGELICA (starting from Fersen).

Not in this dress—my wedding-dress—his bride! Let me change it!

FERSEN.

What matter? There is no time, dearest; I cannot lose you now.

ANGELICA.

Take me as you will; my heart has spoken, not my conscience. It were better I had died than endure this torture. False—false! let the world scorn me as I deserve!

(Fersen leads her out, clinging half helplessly on his arm.)

LADY MARGARET.

Gone! That man's wife—my rival no longer!

(Enter Strossman from library.)

STROSSMAN.

Ah, Lady Margaret, the magic touch! this harpsichord of a woman's heart.

LADY MARGARET.

It was a hard fight; and though I have won, I pity her.

STROSSMAN.

Ah, a fine nature vanquished! Helpless at my feet—full zest of pleasure—in a few hours she will cling to me for consolation.

LADY MARGARET.

But her husband—the powerful Count de Horne?

STROSSMAN.

Her husband, but never in his arms. She will quickly spurn him with contempt and scorn. The wheels are moving quickly now. Go to Sir Joshua, play your game with skill — sympathetic deprecation, not hard blame.

Men are often won in these sudden revulsions of feeling.
The love-motive once stirred in the heart is not easily put
to rest.

LADY MARGARET.

Sir Joshua is painting my portrait—I have a sitting
to-morrow morning.

STROSSMAN.

Why, Fortune is playing your game! A clever touch of
sympathy, and his heart will fall into your hands.

LADY MARGARET.

You are a magician of the heart.

STROSSMAN.

Call me a magician when Angelica is mine. Till to-
morrow, fair lady.

(Strossman goes out.)

LADY MARGARET.

Tender, sympathetic; a favourable impression in the
first hour of disappointment, deepening more and more,
till the torn tendrils of love cling to a new support. Excellent device!

(Rings; servant enters.)

My carriage.

(Exit servant.)

And then hey for Leicester Square! Shall I reign there
in place of the deposed Queen of Hearts? It's a splendid
chance, and I'll use it with my best skill.

(Servant enters, and announces : "Miss Reynolds, my lady!" Miss
Reynolds enters, and servant withdraws.)

MISS REYNOLDS.

There's no mistake about Joshua now; he's over head
and ears at last. He's sent me with these flowers.
Angelica's to wear them to-night in her white dress. It's
a new scheme of colour he wants to study. The idea

flashed into his head as we were going home. The very
thought of her seems to bring fresh inspirations. So,
hey, presto! I'm sent with the flowers while he paints Dr.
Johnson. The Doctor is growling away like a caged bear,
but, bless you! Joshua only smiles, for he can't hear the
growls. Growls and smiles, it will make a grand picture
between them—very brown and rich, like your old sherry
wine. But where's Angelica?

LADY MARGARET.

Miss Kauffmann has left the house.

MISS REYNOLDS.

What a bother! I can't stay; I'm responsible for the
dinner, and the great Doctor will growl all the more if the
dinner goes wrong. Oh, by-the-bye, have you heard the
last bit of gossip? Why, that young Count de Horne
who has been flashing about town is no Count after all!
He has deceived everybody at the Swedish Embassy with
false papers; borrowed money on false pretences—a vulgar
impostor!

LADY MARGARET.

Impossible!

MISS REYNOLDS.

They are after him now—warrants are out. Count
Strossman is my authority. He told me so, as I was
entering the house.

LADY MARGARET (aside).

Then the wheels do move quickly!

MISS REYNOLDS.

Did Angelica go out with her father?

LADY MARGARET.

No.

MISS REYNOLDS.

Alone, then?

LADY MARGARET.

Yes—I mean—I suppose——

MISS REYNOLDS.

What do you mean?

LADY MARGARET.

I can conceal the cruel truth no longer. I am over-whelmed with grief and shame—I can scarcely speak the hateful words—that wicked, deceitful woman has been false to your brother!

MISS REYNOLDS.

Angelica false to Joshua! It will kill him!

LADY MARGARET.

You must not meet her again, dear Miss Reynolds!

MISS REYNOLDS.

False to Joshua! I must get home to him—I must be with him when the blow falls.

(Enter servant.)

SERVANT.

Your ladyship's carriage!

LADY MARGARET.

Let us go at once; that false woman has entrusted me with a cruel message for your brother.

MISS REYNOLDS.

You are a dear, good woman! I can see by your tears that you feel for poor Joshua.

LADY MARGARET.

Indeed I do, Miss Reynolds, from the depth of my heart. Rest on my arm.

(Lady Margaret leads out Miss Reynolds, followed by servant. Strossman enters cautiously from library, followed by two Bow Street officers.)

STROSSMAN.

Search that table—Mr. Kauffmann's working table !

(Officers search.)

FIRST OFFICER.

Impressions of the forged seal, your Excellency—drawings of the seal.

STROSSMAN.

Secure them. You'll have to swear where they were discovered.

(Looks out of window.)

Ah, husband and wife ! They return. Here !

(Beckons officers to window.)

You see that man and woman. The man is Fersen, my valet. When I give the word, you'll arrest him ; here's the warrant. Forgery—the great seal of Sweden ! It's death ! Mark your man ! Now retire.

(Officers go out by library.)

Sir Joshua gone, Fersen arrested, the third lover remains. Ah, Angelica, in the toils now ! I defy you to break the net.

(Goes into library ; Angelica and Fersen enter, ushered in by servant)

ANGELICA.

Has Lady Margaret left the house ?

SERVANT.

Yes, madam, in the carriage.

ANGELICA.

What address did she give ?

SERVANT.

Sir Joshua Reynolds', Leicester Square.

(Servant goes out.)

ANGELICA.

It is well; he will know the truth, and so avoid me from henceforth. His reproaches would kill me!

FERSEN.

Dearest wife, the anguish you suffer is for my sake.

ANGELICA.

Bear with me a little. I have been faithless to my word; it weighs on my conscience; but, believe me,
(With fervour)
I shall be faithless no more, because I love you. Can you trust me?—say, you can trust me?

FERSEN.

My darling wife to-day, by to-morrow's dawn, the noble Countess de Horne!

ANGELICA (with passion).

To-day your wife, to-morrow your wife, your wife to my life's end. I have married *you*—that's my highest honour; not a title, however exalted—married you, since you were free to marry me. But, still, a bride with tears, not smiles, for I am false and perjured, and I have given pain to a noble heart. You said you were ready to leave London this afternoon—let's go.

FERSEN.

So suddenly for you—no preparations!

ANGELICA.

I can pack a few things; only, let's leave this hateful city. I tell you, if I meet the man I have wronged, it would kill me. Dearest husband, grant me this prayer;

don't let me linger here another hour. When I am safely away with you, I shall smile again—all is anguish now.

FERSEN.

Be it so, darling wife. In less than an hour the post-horses shall be here, and then for your new home and new honours! Farewell, sweet one.

(Kisses her forehead.)

ANGELICA.

Don't be long away, I can't bear your absence; a sickening fear besets me!

FERSEN.

Not many minutes, dearest wife.

(He goes out.)

ANGELICA (sitting at table).

Alone! What a whirl of agony it's been—this room strewn with my falsehoods, liar that I am! Judged now —the still, small voice—faithless, perjured, in whispers.

(In changed tone of resolution.)

No, before Heaven and men, I'll not budge one inch. I don't repent! I love him—my husband, my husband! If punishment must fall on me, I will bear it all for the sake of my love!

(Strossman stands at library door watching Angelica, her head buried in her hands.)

Footsteps! oh, joy!—he returns—he returns!

(Strossman retires by library as Sir Joshua enters.)

And now we fly from London. Back so quickly, dearest?

SIR JOSHUA.

Yes, Angel mine.

ANGELICA (starts up in terror, and gazes on Sir Joshua with dazed countenance).

You here? You have come here? Is it possible? Have you seen Lady Margaret?

SIR JOSHUA.

No.

ANGELICA.

She went to your house !
(Aside.)
Oh, Heaven, not this awful punishment on my sin !

SIR JOSHUA.

We must have crossed one another.

ANGELICA.

Then you don't know——

SIR JOSHUA.

Yes, my poor child, and that's why I have come to you
in your grief.   Your poor father——

ANGELICA.

My father ?

SIR JOSHUA.

Let me hold you in my arms, Angelica—to my heart,
your sure refuge.   Sorrow needs a lover's support !

(He tries to fold his arms round her, but she breaks away from him with
violent effort.)

ANGELICA.

I don't understand.   My father, you say—what of my
father ?

SIR JOSHUA.

Then you haven't heard ?   Arrested on a false charge
—it must be false—of forging the great seal of Sweden !

ANGELICA.

Forging—the seal of Sweden !

SIR JOSHUA.

It's absurd! Of course it can all be explained; but for the time he is in custody. It's a wicked story, my poor darling! They say he was employed to do it by that swindler, the valet Fersen, who calls himself Count de Horne!

(Fersen enters in custody of the two officers. Angelica turns, utters a cry of agony, and exclaims, "My husband!" She falls down in a swoon at the feet of Sir Joshua. Strosaman appears at the door of the library.)

CURTAIN.

ACT IV.

THE VALET'S WIFE.

SCENE I.

Sir Joshua Reynolds' painting-room. Octagonal room, lighted by window, R.; door centre R., half-concealed by a folding-screen; door centre L.—entrance to room from picture-gallery. Chair for sitters raised eighteen inches from floor; easel, table with palettes, brushes, colours, etc.; sofa against centre wall.

Northcote discovered setting palette. Miss Reynolds enters.

MISS REYNOLDS.

Mr. Northcote, is everything ready for Sir Joshua?

NORTHCOTE.

Yes, madam.

MISS REYNOLDS.

He must have no small worries to-day—everything to hand. Is Lady Margaret Forbes' canvas on the easel? Her second sitting, is it not?

NORTHCOTE.

The third. The head is blocked in; I have been at work on the drapery. I have just set Sir Joshua's palette according to his practice, so he will be able to begin painting without delay.

MISS REYNOLDS.

Thank you, Mr. Northcote. You work for a good master.

NORTHCOTE.

Good, and great, Miss Reynolds! I can never do too
much in my insignificant way to help him—he helped me,
a poor lad from Devonshire. "His house is to me a very
paradise!"

(Servant enters L., and announces, "Lady Margaret Forbes." Lady
Margaret enters, and servant withdraws. Northcote goes out door R.)

LADY MARGARET.

Dear Miss Reynolds, I have kept my appointment with
Sir Joshua, not having received any intimation to the con-
trary; but surely he will not work to-day!

MISS REYNOLDS.

He will—he will!

LADY MARGARET.

But so soon after the conduct of that heartless jilt—a
woman so unworthy of his love!

MISS REYNOLDS.

He says the brush is his best consoler—and after the
brush, his sister Fanny. I wish, for his sake, that I were
only half as good as a brush.

LADY MARGARET.

He loved her so deeply—what does he say?—his just
indignation at such vile conduct.

MISS REYNOLDS.

He says nothing. I only wish he would speak and have
it out; I think silence will break his heart.

LADY MARGARET.

Silent—even with you?

MISS REYNOLDS.

Her name is never to be mentioned again in this house. That is all he said when he returned home. He was very quiet and thoughtful all last evening, but I heard him mutter from time to time, " Poor woman ! what a fate— what a fate !"

LADY MARGARET.

A man so deeply wronged!

MISS REYNOLDS.

Alas! and a woman so deeply loved. I can't understand him. I should have been furious! I don't pretend to understand him, but something tells me that, with all his greatness, he was never greater than he is now. Don't speak or allude to her—I think it would kill him. I will tell him you are here, and then I must go my daily round of housekeeping. It's very strange, no break in the circle —trot, trot—the donkey at the wheel : the world always eats, sorrow or joy. He has sent to invite his old cronies to dinner to-day—the great Doctor, and poor Goldie, who missed their dinners yesterday, and Mr. Burke. He bears it so bravely, I only pray Heaven he mayn't break down ; but it's hard to bear, even for a resolute man. Farewell, dear Lady Margaret.

(Goes out R.)

LADY MARGARET.

Farewell, dear Miss Reynolds. And now to play my game—cool, cautious, subtle. He clings to love, that's clear. It only remains to efface one impression from the heart by substituting another—love the passion, then a simple transference ; it should be very easy with an easy, pleasant-going man.

(Sir Joshua enters R.)

SIR JOSHUA.

Good-morning, Lady Margaret. Most punctual! A great lady who keeps strict appointment with an artist—it's a marvel!

LADY MARGARET.

But you know my love of art, Sir Joshua, my admiration. It leads me, I fear, to waste my time in hopeless striving to be an artist myself; but, at least, it enables me to sympathize with artists and their labours, and their grand aspirations. My poor painting-room at home is my happiness from morning to night.

SIR JOSHUA.

Ah, admiration—fervour of soul! I like that expression—it suits your face. Let's catch it ere it flies. Take your seat, my lady.

(She sits.)

So; excellent attitude!—natural, elegant! Ah, you say you love art and artists?

LADY MARGARET.

With enthusiasm!

SIR JOSHUA (painting).

The fine artistic glow! Excellent! The sustaining spirit with which we must encounter difficulties and overcome them. And art is difficult—pain and hard labour—ideals which are never satisfied, bright hopes which die away in sorrow.

LADY MARGARET.

I should rejoice to suffer for a high purpose—a grand ideal.

SIR JOSHUA (painting intently).

Good! good! Noble sentiments for travellers on the thorny road of art.

(Becomes absorbed in work.)

Ah me! many are called, but few are chosen—few, very few.

LADY MARGARET (aside).

Fair progress, and assurance of my love for art, and then an imperceptible substitution of the new love for the old, both in the same guise; a masquerade of hearts, perhaps, but all life is a masquerade.

(Aloud.)

Shall you go to the masked ball at the Pantheon rooms, Sir Joshua? They say it will be so grand—all the rank and fashion. I love to see the fancy dresses—they always look like subjects for a picture—one wants to group them. Sir Joshua, I asked—Sir Joshua! He does not hear; I'll try another subject. Sir Joshua, were not the Venetians the greatest colourists? Intent on the canvas, but he never looks at me. Sir Joshua, I was asking—— Deaf, or he won't listen. May I see your method of laying on the colours? Only a moment. No answer; I'll take the liberty on myself.

(She leaves her seat, and steals up behind Sir Joshua, who does not perceive her.)

Why, that's not my face! it's Angelica's face, every feature —Angelica. A striking likeness. That woman! Why, this is a positive insult to me!

(Aloud.)

Sir Joshua!

(He starts.)

Sir Joshua, you are not painting my portrait!

SIR JOSHUA (arousing himself from his reverie).

Eh? Your portrait? Yes—yes, my dear lady—yes. Oh, I see, I've missed the expression; it's all got wrong and muddled.

(Calls.)

Northcote! Northcote!

(He sinks into a chair, clasping his hands over his face. Northcote enters R., and comes up to Sir Joshua.)

NORTHCOTE.

Yes, Sir Joshua.

(Places his hand on Sir Joshua's shoulder; Sir Joshua starts up.)

SIR JOSHUA.

Take that canvas away, it's spoilt; scrape it out; bring me a fresh canvas.

(Northcote goes out L. with the canvas.)

Pardon me, Lady Margaret.

(Bows.)

We'll set to work again. So you really love art, and artists, and painting-rooms? Good—very good! Oh, you said the Pantheon. I shall be there. I love the bright, dazzling sight, the music and the dances. The honour of one dance, Lady Margaret, if I'm not too old a partner, and if I am fortunate enough to discover you under a mask.

(Bows. Northcote enters L., carrying canvas.)

Here's Northcote; now to work.

NORTHCOTE.

Sir Joshua, a lady insists upon seeing you. She will take no denial. It's imperative, she declares. I believe it is Miss Kauffmann; indeed, I'm sure it is her figure.

SIR JOSHUA (deeply agitated).

I will not see her—I will not see her.

NORTHCOTE (listening at door L.).

She's coming upstairs—they can't keep her out.

SIR JOSHUA.

Lady Margaret, I must leave you. If that woman insists upon entering this room, you must tell her that I have left the house. My sister is not at home, I must ask you to dismiss her—firmly, not harshly. She ought to know that I cannot see her.

(He goes out R. Northcote goes to door L. Sounds without of expostulation; voice of Angelica: "I say I must see him!" Angelica enters, her face partly concealed by a veil.)

ANGELICA.

Where's Sir Joshua ?

LADY MARGARET.

He has left the house, madam; your strange intrusion
has driven him away. How can you have the audacity
to venture here—the house of the man you have so shame-
fully deceived ?

(Sir Joshua re-enters room, and remains concealed behind screen.)

ANGELICA.

Despair has brought me. You have driven me from
your door. All doors are closed against me. I am alone.
I know not where to turn for help. My husband in prison,
my father in prison; Bartolozzi has left London in alarm.
My father is to be brought up for examination this morning. No friend to speak for him. The lying accusation is
so strong, so horribly strong, he will be committed for
trial. It will kill him—kill him! Sir Joshua's word for
his character might alter everything—save him from this
disgrace.

LADY MARGARET.

Shameless woman! You dare to come to Sir Joshua to
beg for his help after deliberately breaking your plighted
word, after marrying an impostor, a weaver of forgeries
and lies !

ANGELICA.

It is false! My husband is no impostor; he is the
victim of deception.

LADY MARGARET.

The testimony of the Swedish Embassy, Count Strossman——

ANGELICA.

The forgeries and lies are his devilish invention !

LADY MARGARET.

Incredible story !

7

ANGELICA.

I have not come here to excuse my conduct, or even to attempt it; but thus much I can urge : Count Strossman has long pursued me with dishonour. One fatal night he held me in his toils—a helpless, unsuspecting woman—lured me to his house. Alone, with a drugged cup prepared; sleep, drugged helpless sleep, was to have delivered me, an unresisting victim, into his vile power—shame and disgrace! I stand here an honourable woman, because the man I have married risked everything—life itself, in spite of the contempt and scorn I had heaped upon him in my blindness, to save me from this fate worse than death. He is in prison, and I am alone and helpless; but that vile wretch pursues me still with his loathsome suit, with his hypocritical offers of sympathy and help. In this house at least I am safe from insult and outrage.

LADY MARGARET.

An improbable story! What night?

ANGELICA.

That supper-night after the play.

LADY MARGARET.

Ridiculous invention! An outrage in the presence of a large company of guests! I was present myself. A clear tissue of lies!

(Sir Joshua comes forward from behind screen.)

Sir Joshua, I regret to say that this heartless woman has the effrontery to linger here. She has told me some absurd story which, on the face of it, is false.

SIR JOSHUA.

I heard the story, my lady;—I believe it.

(Angelica sinks to the ground.)

Lady Margaret, I must ask you to postpone this sitting; I

find I am not in a state to do justice to your portrait.
Forgive me, I must wish you good-morning.

(Calls.)

Mr. Northcote!

(Northcote enters.)

Lady Margaret Forbes! Will you see her ladyship to her carriage?

LADY MARGARET.

Am I to leave you—leave you with this false, heartless woman?

(Sir Joshua makes no reply, but stands gazing on Angelica.)

Deaf! The fool! he loves her still. I should like to tell him. Useless—deaf, or won't hear. My scheme breaks down; my game of love has been played in vain.

(Follows Northcote out of the room. A pause.)

SIR JOSHUA (in voice of great restraint).

Rest assured I will do all in my power to help your father, of whose innocence there can be no question. I will go at once to Bow Street with my own attorney. A new light breaks upon me. Count Strossman! There may indeed have been foul play—foul, disgraceful purpose! I'll search it out; the guilty shall not escape!

ANGELICA (in low, broken tones).

I dare not speak to you—I dare not speak.

SIR JOSHUA.

I dare not listen to your voice.

(Northcote enters.)

Mr. Northcote, will you please to order a coach for this lady.

(Northcote bows, and goes out.)

I would have you remember these last words which end all intercourse between us. I have not judged you in bitterness, but in sorrow; I have not judged you hastily, because I believed that your nature was too noble to be guilty of petty meanness and deception; I felt assured that there must have been a great and terrible struggle in your soul before you failed in loyalty to me ; and, I thank God, I felt assured of this in that first hour of dismay and sorrow.

> (Pause.)

Farewell.   I would that it had been mine to stand where that young man stood on that shameful night.

> (Northcote enters.)

Mr. Northcote will see you to your coach.   Return home. I will do my best to restore your father to you.

> (He retires slowly into room R. Angelica, raising herself, gazes after him in silence, and then, uttering a sigh of deep emotion, she takes Northcote's arm ; he leads her toward door L.)

END OF SCENE I.

SCENE II.

A room in Angelica's house in Golden Square, ground-floor ; window C., looking out into the Square through the iron railings of the area (practical behind railings). Door of room L., opening into the hall passage ; key in door. The room is in confusion, partly furnished ; some of the furniture is covered up with dusting-sheets.

Angelica enters in great excitement, followed by an old servant.

ANGELICA.

Sheriff's officers in the house ? Impossible ! When did they come ?

SERVANT.

Half an hour ago. They forced their way in, when I opened the door !

ANGELICA.

How dare they ? It must be some mistake. I have no debts. Let me see the men.

> (Servant goes to door. Sheriff's officer enters.)

What is the meaning of this ?

OFFICER.

Seizure of goods and chattels, ma'am, at the suit of Moss Levi.

ANGELICA.

But I owe the man nothing. This is my house, my furniture.

OFFICER.

Yes, ma'am, and therefore it is your husband's house and furniture; they must pay his debts.

ANGELICA.

Infamous!

OFFICER.

It's the law, ma'am; here's the writ!

(Offers writ.)

ANGELICA.

Is there no refuge left for me?
(To servant.)
Go to Mr. Bartolozzi's—find him somehow, somewhere; I must see him at once. Tell him I have no friend—no friend to help me. Go! go!

(Exit servant.)

OFFICER.

Don't ye take on, ma'am; friends turn up when least expected. A handsome young woman has always lots of friends; so cheer up, my pretty lady, cheer up!

ANGELICA.

Silence, man! Do your work, but don't address me.

OFFICER.

Hoity toity! No offence—no offence!
(Knock at street-door.)
There's a knock! A friend at last, I'll be bound.
(Calls out into passage.)
Open the door, Bill, servant's out. Show the visitor in—proper style, like a cove in plush. Bless me, ma'am, we often does the plush-and-powder business—it's all in the day's work.

ANGELICA.

It's Bartolozzi, I trust. How could he have deserted me at such a time? No doubt the fear of that accusation. But it's very cowardly; he ought to have stood side by side with my poor father, for he led him into this terrible difficulty.

(Strossman enters.)

You here? You dare to enter my house? Go, I say!

STROSSMAN.

Listen to me. I feared this seizure would take place. I knew that your property is the property of that impostor, liable to the last penny for his debts. These men shall not molest you; I will free you from their presence.

(To officer.)

What is the amount of the debt?

(Officer shows writ; Strossman takes ont notes, which he counts,
　　　and gives to officer.)

Count them, and go!

(Officer counts notes.)

OFFICER.

Said a friend was bound to turn up, ma'am; pretty faces have always lots of friends!

STROSSMAN.

Begone, fellow, at once!

ANGELICA.

No, stay—stay!

(Flies to officer.)

I pray you to remain as long as that man remains in the house!

OFFICER.

Must go, ma'am—debt's paid; no legal right to stay another minute; action for trespass would lie against Sheriff. Good-morning, pretty lady, you're in luck— lovers who pay like that!

(Officer goes ont.)

ANGELICA.

Will you go, or will you stay ? Answer me.

STROSSMAN.

Stay awhile, with your permission ; I have something to say.

ANGELICA.

Keep your distance ! I shall go, if you dare to approach me !

STROSSMAN.

Go, madam, you are free to go—you are free to treat me with insolence and scorn—to treat me as if I were a vulgar bully, capable of using brute force against a woman. Contemptible thought ! Mental force is my method, not vulgar muscle. You are free to go, I say, free to forget that your father stands accused of serious crime.

ANGELICA.

Innocent !

STROSSMAN.

Let him prove it with the damning proof which stands against him. Red-handed is his guilt—the forged seal concealed in his pocket. Let him prove it, I say. But if the accusation be pressed home, as I can press it, his chances of escape are small.

ANGELICA.

Merciful Heaven ! And you will—you will ?

STROSSMAN.

Pray retire, madam ; you desire to go ; I shall not raise one finger to detain you. And that arch impostor who has so cruelly deceived you, deceived us all— one tissue of lies and forgeries !

ANGELICA.

You liar ! It's false, I say !

STROSSMAN.

You say! What's the worth of your word? Impetuosity and violence are no proofs! If the charges be pressed home, it's death to that man—to two men, that impostor and your father. Go, madam! I say so with reason; the debt I have just discharged transfers this house to me, till you can acquit the debt.

(Silence.)

ANGELICA.

But if it were not pressed—not pressed ?

STROSSMAN.

They might escape the law. But if the evidence to be given against my late valet to-morrow is actually given, he will be committed for trial, and I shall be bound over to prosecute.

ANGELICA.

And you will ?

STROSSMAN.

I must! He will be tried. The penalty of forgery is death.

ANGELICA.

Innocent, I repeat, innocent!

STROSSMAN.

Evidence, not innocence. I will not detain you; it is useless to prolong this interview.

(Sits.)

ANGELICA (approaching him).

But you will not ? you cannot ? .
(Falling on her knees.)
I pray you by all that's sacred—as a daughter, as a wife—have mercy on a woman, a miserable woman !

STROSSMAN (aside).

" By to-morrow morning, on her knees !"
(Aloud.)
Madam, I have my public duty to consider, pray leave

me; it is useless to strive thus; the law must have its course. This interview is too painful; if you decline to go, it must be for me to leave this house.

(He rises from chair; she rises.)

ANGELICA.

Not before a promise—give me a promise.
(Takes his hands.)
Their lives—their lives !

STROSSMAN *(withdrawing his hands).*

Their lives—you beg their lives ?

ANGELICA.

I beg and pray—with tears—with a breaking heart !

STROSSMAN.

I cannot answer your prayer now. If you choose to renew this interview, you are at liberty to come to my house in Chelsea at ten o'clock this evening; I will then consider what I may do to help you. Here is a private key—the garden entrance.

(Offers key, which she flings down.)

ANGELICA.

Vile wretch ! inhuman monster ! Oh, accursed bargain ! —my honour or their lives !

STROSSMAN.

You will pick up the key later. No need for these heroics—you come, or you stay away, the choice is with you—their lives ! Farewell, madam, or au revoir—as you will.

(She casts herself in an agony of despair on the sofa; he goes to door, turns, and contemplates her. Aside.)

Victory at last ! At ten o'clock to-night she will come. I have won, my Lady Margaret !

(Turns to door, and is about to go out, when Fersen staggers into the room. Strossman slinks back towards window. Fersen locks the door, and secures key in his pocket; staggers to a chair—he is out of breath, panting with exhaustion. Angelica rises from the sofa with a cry, and, kneeling, clasps him in her arms.)

ANGELICA.

Husband!—free!

FERSEN (in broken tones).

I have escaped from the guard. A long chase—I outran them; but I fear they are on my traces. I fled here. The street-door was on the latch; I've locked and bolted it. Breathing time! But in a few minutes they will tear me away! Oh, Angelica, my wife, how dare I meet you? I have been deceived—I am not the deceiver. Deceived by that scoundrel Strossman, I married you as Count de Horne. The forgeries were his—his revenge for that night of infamy when I saved you from outrage and shame!

ANGELICA.

I guessed the truth. That evil hand!

FERSEN.

Oh wife, deeply wronged, let me gaze in your eyes, and tell me you still have faith in my honour!

ANGELICA.

Husband, dearest husband, my faith has never wavered.

FERSEN.

Bless you for those words! Oh, noble woman, you have made me strong again—Fersen, the valet! But love and honour were mine—the wrong was not mine. If I live, the wrong shall be avenged on that man's head!

STROSSMAN (coming forward).

Lying impostor! you will not live.

FERSEN (starts to his feet).

You here—here, in this room with her, my wife! Some new outrage—the purpose of your vile scheme! Revenge is in my hands! Caged! I have the key! Better for you a lion's den than my anger and my wrongs!

STROSSMAN.

Fool! in a few minutes——

FERSEN.

Then minutes are precious!
(He flies on Strossman ; Strossman struggles to window.)

STROSSMAN (at window, breaking panes of glass).

Help! The scoundrel Fersen is in this room! Help!
help!

(Fersen drags Strossman back from window, and flings him on his
knees.)

FERSEN.

Speak again, and I'll tear the tongue from your lying
throat!

STROSSMAN.

They've heard! They were watching the house!
(Rises, and draws his sword.)

My prisoner! they will break into this room and drag you
away.
(Aloud to crowd which gathers at railings.)

Help! Tell them to smash in the doors!
(Strossman keeps off Fersen with his sword.)

Yes; my scheme the forged seal, my scheme the impos-
ture—I avow it—my scheme to conquer that proud
woman; and I've won!

FERSEN.

He confesses the foul plot—vile wretch!

ANGELICA.

I shall declare it before the world—his own confession!
(To Fersen.)

You are saved!

STROSSMAN.

A wife's evidence is of no avail—no one else has heard
my words. I'm no fool. Mine, I say, or your husband
will be hanged from the front of Newgate!

ANGELICA.

Fiend incarnate!   Oh, Heaven! can such things be?

STROSSMAN.

Ay; I'm master of life and death!

(Murmur of crowd, and voice without: " Open, iu the King's namo!" Crash of street-door being forced.)

Time is short; bid your fair wife farewell, and leave her in my charge!

(Fersen tries to close with him.)

Keep your distance, man, or I shall save the hangman's work!

(In loud voice.)

Murder! murder!   Help! help!

(Noise and voices at door of room. Voice without : "Open, in the King's namo!" Fersen catches up chair, rushes on Strossman, breaks sword out of his hand, catches up sword, then turns and confronts Stross-man. Strossman, in terror :)

Help! quick!   Murder!

(To Fersen.)

You will be hanged, if you injure me!

FERSEN.

A man can die but once.   A life for a life—it's quits now.   Oh, vile monster! they will be too late to save you! Death by my hands!   Prepare—death at the moment the door is broken!

(Blows on the door, which shakes under the strokes.)

STROSSMAN.

Help! help! murder!   Break down the door!

(A panel of the door is broken, the pieces flying into the room.)

FERSEN (in loud voice).

Hold your hands!   Another blow, and this man dies before your eyes!

(To Strossman.)

Tell them to hold their hands, if you want to live!

STROSSMAN.

Officers, hold your hands, I beg and pray!

FERSEN.

Pray! you shall pray! Scoundrel, down on your knees before the woman you have wronged!

(Angelica has sunk back dazed into chair.)

Obey, man, or, by Heaven! you die. To your knees, I say!

(Strossman falls on his knees, facing Angelica and the door.)

Pray? No; confession before absolution! Confess the blackness of your soul before Heaven and men! Speak! or one quick thrust and you die! Speak!

(In low tone, prompting Strossman.)

"I fabricated the story of Fersen being Count de Horne."

(Aloud.)

Speak, man!

STROSSMAN (in low tone).

"I fabricated the story of Fersen being Count de Horne."

FERSEN.

Louder, I say! Repeat the words. Let all honest men listen to your shame.

STROSSMAN (raising his voice).

"I fabricated the story of Fersen being Count de Horne."

FERSEN.

Tell the infamous story of your forgeries—quickly, or, by Heaven, you die!

STROSSMAN.

I forged the royal decree; I forged the Ambassador's signature to the direction for a new seal.

FERSEN.

Go on!

STROSSMAN.

I found moneys for Fersen's dress and expenses, and I had him arrested for debt—arrested as an impostor and a forger.

FERSEN.

Why did you do this wickedness—why, I say? Answer, or I'll wring the vile truth from your accursed throat. Why?

STROSSMAN.

That I might force this lady to listen to my dishonourable suit.

FERSEN. *

Confession black enough! Now pray—pray this lady's pardon for the grievous wrong.

STROSSMAN.

Madam, I humbly crave your pardon!

FERSEN.

Pray to her mercy for your vile life!

STROSSMAN.

Save me—save me, O gracious lady!

ANGELICA (in a low voice).

Spare him.

FERSEN.

Enough; your life is spared.

(He flings down sword, unlocks door, throws it open.)

I submit to the law.

(Bow Street officers enter, followed by the Swedish Ambassador, Sir Joshua Reynolds, and Kauffmann, who goes to his daughter and embraces her, and afterwards by Miss Reynolds.)

STROSSMAN (aside).

The Ambassador! I'm lost!

(To Ambassador.)

I trust that your Excellency will give no heed to words forced from my lips at the point of the sword.

AMBASSADOR.

Count Strossman, you will at once report yourself at the Embassy. The truth of your confession will be closely tested. I suspect you have certain accomplices; they will be examined forthwith. With regard to this young man, unfortunate, and deeply wronged, I believe ; I will accept the undertaking of any responsible person for his appearance at the Embassy when required. Meantime, the charges against him are withdrawn.

SIR JOSHUA.

I accept the responsibility of Mr. Fersen's appearance.

AMBASSADOR.

Your word, Sir Joshua, is amply sufficient. Count Strossman, you had better follow me ; the inquiry must proceed at once.

(Ambassador, bowing to Sir Joshua, goes out.)

STROSSMAN (aside).

Lost, in the moment of triumph—the promise of a life wrecked! Madness! A great career—only a woman !

(About to go.)

FERSEN.

Do not let us meet again, Count Strossman. I have given you your life that this lady's honour and my own might be vindicated by truth wrung from your vile lips ; but the next time we meet it will be short shrift and sure death !

(Strossman goes out. To Angelica)

And now, O lady deeply loved, and yet cruelly wronged in innocence by me, I make the last reparation in my power. I shall leave this country, as soon as the law permits. Your husband, but in name—the marriage of a Protestant with a Catholic—I am told that the law will grant you an easy divorce. You will be free, and I pray that the recollection of the valet Fersen may pass away from your memory like the trouble of an evil dream. He will bear with him a great sorrow—haply not for long, for some wounds of the heart never heal, and the life-blood ebbs silently away. And yet, with all that weight of sorrow, he will possess the happiness of a conscience devoid of all guilt towards the woman he has so deeply loved and honoured.

KAUFFMANN (going up to Fersen).

Young man, you have made the best reparation in your
power; I forgive you.

(Clasps his hand.)

My daughter free !

ANGELICA.

No, father, for ever no ! Bound by holy ordinance—
bound by all that can bind a woman's heart : respect for
a man's nobleness and honour; sympathy for noble and
unmerited suffering !

FERSEN.

The valet Fersen !

ANGELICA.

No, my husband—the husband of Angelica Kauffmann !

(To Fersen.)

You would have raised me to your estate—the honours of
a great kingdom ; I raise you to mine—the kingdom of
art, my honoured husband !

(She clasps him in her arms.)

SIR JOSHUA (to Kauffmann).

She has spoken well, Mr. Kauffmann ; I honour her.
Good-bye.

(Turns to go.)

MISS REYNOLDS (clasping Sir Joshua's hands).

Dear, good, noble Joshua !

SIR JOSHUA.

Dear, foolish sister Fanny ! Nay, we must be getting
home ; Dr. Johnson will be waiting.

(Takes Miss Reynolds' arm : they turn to go.)

CURTAIN.

BILLING AND SONS, PRINTERS, GUILDFORD.
J. D. & Co.